Sw

Made in Savannah
Cozy Mystery Series Book Four

Hope Callaghan

hopecallaghan.com
Copyright © 2016
All rights reserved.

This book is a work of fiction. Although places mentioned may be real, the characters, names and incidents, and all other details are products of the author's imagination and are fictitious. Any resemblance to actual events or actual persons, living or dead is purely coincidental.

No part of this publication may be copied, reproduced in any format, by any means, electronic or otherwise, without prior consent from the copyright owner and publisher of this book. The only exception is brief quotations in printed reviews.

Visit my website for new releases and special offers: hopecallaghan.com

Special Thanks

Thank you to these wonderful ladies who help make my books shine - Peggy H., Cindi G., Jean P., Wanda D., Rosmarie H. and Barbara W. for taking the time to preview *Swag in Savannah,* for the extra sets of eyes and for catching all my mistakes.

A special thanks to my reader review team: Alice, Amary, Barbara, Becky, Becky B, Brinda, Cassie, Christina, Cyndi, Debbie, Denota, Devan, Francine, Grace, Jan, Jo-Ann, Joeline, Joyce, Jean K., Jean M., Kathy, Lynne, Megan, Melda, Kat, Linda, Lynne, Pat, Patsy, Paula, Renate, Rita, Rita P, Shelba, Tamara and Vicki

TABLE OF CONTENTS

Special Thanks.. ii

Like Free Books?... v

Chapter 1 1

Chapter 2 15

Chapter 3 25

Chapter 4 40

Chapter 5 49

Chapter 6 65

Chapter 7 78

Chapter 8 92

Chapter 9 109

Chapter 10 127

Chapter 11 146

Chapter 12 154

Chapter 13 165

Chapter 14 173

Chapter 15	*181*
Chapter 16	*188*
Chapter 17	*205*
Chapter 18	*221*
Chapter 19	*233*
Chapter 20	*241*
Chapter 21	*256*
Chapter 22	*268*
Chapter 23	*281*
Chapter 24	*294*
Chapter 25	*304*
Get Free Books and More	*313*
Meet The Author	*314*
Bow Tie Pasta with Sausage, Tomatoes and Cream Recipe	*315*
Garlucci Family Secret Sicilian Seasoning Recipe	*317*

Like Free Books?

Get Free & Discounted Books, Giveaways & New Releases When You Subscribe To My Free Cozy Mysteries Newsletter!

HopeCallaghan.com/newsletter

Chapter 1

Tony Garlucci wrapped his arms around his mother and hugged her tightly.

Carlita closed her eyes as she hugged him back. She released her grip and took a step back. "Let me look at you. You look good." Carlita touched a wayward strand of hair on the side of his forehead. "Ah, maybe I see a new gray hair or two," she teased her middle son.

"It's good to see you, too, Ma," Tony grinned. He leaned down and greeted Rambo, Carlita's dog. Rambo was nudging Tony's leg, his tail wagging at breakneck speed. "You, too, buddy." Tony had given Rambo to Carlita when they lived in New York, after her son found out someone had broken into her house.

"Have a seat." Carlita motioned him to the dining room chair. "Can I get you a pop? Maybe a water? I just pulled a batch of your favorite cookies out of the oven."

"No Ma," Tony shook his head and eased into one of the chairs. "I'm fine. I have something to tell you."

Carlita dropped into the chair next to her son. By the tone of his voice, she could tell it was serious. "What is it son?"

"It's about Vinnie." Vinnie was Carlita's oldest child and her deceased husband's namesake.

"Is Vinnie okay?"

"Vinnie…is on the lam."

"On the lam?" Carlita shook her head, confused.

"He's on the run," Tony said bluntly. "He gave one of the 'dons' a lousy insider trading tip. The don lost his shirt in some hefty financial transactions thanks to Vinnie's advice and now there's a hit out on him. He's trying to lay low, hoping it'll blow over."

"Don who?" Carlita blinked rapidly.

"You know, a mafia boss. I don't know him personally but he's someone up and coming in the ranks. Never heard the name until a couple months ago but rumor has it he's ruthless."

"Oh, I guess I forgot what that meant," Carlita said. "Do you have any idea where your brother is hiding?"

"Nope and it's probably a good thing." Tony shook his head. "The don's cronies have been tailing me for weeks."

Carlita cut her son off. "You didn't bring them to Savannah?" she gasped. "We're here to escape the mafia, not bring them to us!"

"Nah!" Tony waved a hand. "Least I don't think so. I was gonna book a flight and fly down but figured the don's goons would tail me for sure what with their insider connections and all. I think we're safe," he said confidently.

He changed the subject. "No use worrying about it right now. I'm here to help you set up your pawnshop. Have you come up with a name?"

Carlita's brow furrowed. "I want something catchy, something that's going to draw in customers who're curious to see our unique items and one-of-a-kind wares."

Mercedes, who had been listening in on the conversation between her mother and brother, leaned her hip against the side of the kitchen counter and crossed her arms. "Mobster Marketplace. That's catchy."

"Mobster Marketplace?" Carlita asked. "We might as well call it *We're the Mafia Marketplace*."

"I like that name too." Mercedes reached into the basket of fruit behind her and grabbed an apple.

"What about Savannah Swag?" Tony suggested.

"Hmm. That has a nice ring to it." Carlita clapped her hands. "Savannah Swag. I like it! What exactly does swag mean?"

"In the mobster world it means stolen goods."

"Oh! Maybe I don't want to use the name after all. It will give people the wrong impression." Carlita frowned. "Our goods won't be stolen. We'll be procuring our inventory on the up and up."

"It's still a cool name." Mercedes took a big bite of apple and chewed loudly. "If nothing else, people will be curious and come into the store just to see what kind of hot goods we're trying to move."

Carlita shook her head. "Not to mention the local police. Do we want to set ourselves up for that kind of attention?"

"I think the name is perfect," Tony said.

They tossed out a few other suggestions but none of them was as catchy as *Savannah Swag* so they unanimously decided it would be the official name of their new pawnshop.

Carlita popped out of her chair and set her empty tea glass on the counter before turning to Tony. "Are you ready for a tour of Savannah Swag?"

Tony, Mercedes and Carlita wandered into the hall and down the apartment steps where Carlita unlocked the back door to what would be the pawnshop and flipped the light switch. The trio stepped inside.

"This is it?" Tony gazed around the back room.

"No. Follow me." Carlita led the way into the spacious front of the shop. The smell of fresh paint and floor varnish lingered in the air.

Tony strolled to the center of the room, stuck his hands in his front pockets and spun in a slow circle. "Not too shabby," he said as he gazed up at the exposed industrial-size vents and ceiling rafters. "I like the industrial look. It fits."

Carlita shared her plans with Tony, her idea for the store layout.

"Where you gonna get the goods?" Tony asked. "I got some thoughts on where we can find merchandise."

"Only if they're purchased legally," Carlita said. "I don't want any hot goods, fenced goods or...swag. You know what I mean - *illegal* swag."

"There are legit places to purchase items," Tony said. "Don't worry. I won't get you into any trouble."

They discussed several ideas for logistics, transporting goods, advertising and cash flow. Carlita was impressed by her son's business acumen.

Tony's excitement over the new business endeavor was contagious and as they talked, Carlita could envision the business up and running. "So you'll stay until we have the doors open and the kinks worked out?"

"Say you'll stay," Mercedes said. "We need all the help we can get."

Tony looked at his mother and sister. "All right. I'll help. I've always wanted to see how the other side of a business ran. I might as well take a look at the other properties, too."

"They still need a lot of work," Carlita warned. "Follow me."

The three exited through the front door and turned right. They stopped in front of the courtyard gate that separated the pawnshop from their second property.

Tony took a quick look through the bars before they continued on to what Carlita hoped would one day be her Italian restaurant.

Carlita unlocked the front door of the empty building and they stepped inside.

Tony stopped near a faint chalk outline. "Is this where Vinnie found the broad's body?"

Vinnie, Carlita's oldest son, along with Carlita, Mercedes and their friend Autumn Winter, had discovered a body inside the old restaurant the day they arrived in Savannah to move into their new home.

The body belonged to Norma Jean Cleaver, one of the Savannah Architectural Society members. It had been a bumpy start to their new life in Savannah. Carlita, with some help from her daughter and Autumn, had uncovered the killer and cleared Carlita's name.

"Yeah. That's where we found her." Carlita ran the tip of her shoe over the mark. "I need to get in here and at least clean the floor."

The trio toured the rest of the property before wandering out the back door to the alley that ran behind the building. They looped all the way around until they reached the side of what would soon be the pawnshop.

Tony stopped abruptly. He pointed at a set of street level rectangular windows. Thick wrought iron bars covered the windows. "You got a basement? I haven't seen it yet."

"Me either. I asked Bob Bowman, our construction supervisor, about it. He thinks the access to the basement is either in the old restaurant or maybe the storage unit on the other side of the restaurant." A cold chill ran through Carlita and she rubbed the tops of her arms. "The windows look kinda creepy."

After they were safely inside, Carlita locked the door behind them and tugged on the handle to make sure it had locked. "One of the neighborhood business owners said he could've sworn he saw someone walking around inside here in the wee hours of the morning so I've been making my rounds each night to make sure the place is secure."

"Autumn works at the Savannah Evening News. She told us she ran across an old article about this place. At one time, it was a casket-making factory. My theory is the neighbor saw a ghost," Mercedes said.

"Ghosts schmosts," Tony teased. "You always have had a vivid imagination." He ruffled his sister's hair and Mercedes stuck her tongue out at him.

"Okay. Break it up you two," Carlita joked. "Let's head upstairs and I'll fix lunch."

Tony, who had followed his sister into the back room, stopped abruptly. "What you gonna do with this space?"

"Storage?" Carlita shrugged. "I haven't given it much thought."

Mercedes eased past her brother. "There's a separate bathroom over here. We could fix up the kitchenette and then section off the other side to carve out a studio apartment."

"Ah." Carlita raised a brow. "That's an idea. I hadn't thought of that. What do you think Tony?"

"Meh." Tony rubbed the stubble on his chin. "It has potential. Waste not, want not. I'd squeeze every buck out of this place I could get." He walked over to the dilapidated kitchen area, opened the front doors of the cupboard and peered inside. "This old cabinet will pop right out. You could easily rehab it."

He tilted his head as he studied the interior of the cabinet before shifting his gaze. "I see somethin' in here. You got a flashlight I can borrow?"

"Sure," Carlita said.

"I'll get it." Mercedes darted out of the room, her quick steps thumping loudly on the stairs as she headed to their apartment on the second floor. She returned a short time later, flashlight in hand. "Here."

"Thanks." Tony grabbed the flashlight, switched it on and pointed the light at the floor. "There's something in here." He angled the flashlight and studied the frame of the cabinet. "I need a screwdriver or an electric drill."

Mercedes groaned. "You're really working me here, bro." She darted out of sight and quickly returned with a set of screwdrivers and a drill. "I brought both."

Tony grabbed the electric drill and crawled into the cabinet. "Hold the light." His voice echoed from the interior of the cabinet.

Carlita reached for the flashlight and adjusted the beam to illuminate the inside of the cabinet.

ZIP-ZIP. The buzz of the drill vibrated the frame.

"I think I got it." Tony eased out of the cabinet and jumped to his feet. "Grab hold of the other side and we'll pull it away from the wall."

The trio grabbed the front and side of the cabinet. With a few firm tugs, they were able to pull it away from the wall. After they dragged it across the floor and eased it against the wall, they returned to the now empty corner.

Carlita lowered her gaze and studied the floor where the cabinet had been. There was a large, square cutout. At one end was a round brass ring. "What is that?"

Mercedes peeked around her mother's shoulder. "It looks like some sort of access panel."

Chapter 2

"Stand back." Tony motioned them back before he knelt down, grabbed the round ring and pulled hard. "It ain't budgin'."

"It's nailed shut." Mercedes pointed at the edges of the cutout. Sure enough, it appeared someone had nailed the cutout to the floor.

"I need a crowbar," Tony said.

Mercedes snorted and rolled her eyes.

"I'll get it. Tell me where it's at," Tony said.

"I'll get it but I'm gonna start charging you," Mercedes threatened as she stomped up the stairs. The apartment door slammed. A short time later, she stomped back down the steps. "Here." She thrust the crowbar into her brother's hand.

"Thanks. Since you brought me all the tools, I'll let you be the first one to check it out."

"I don't think so." Mercedes clutched her chest, her eyes widening in horror.

"He's kidding," Carlita said. "At least I hope your brother is kidding."

Tony resumed his position on the floor. He wedged the tip of the crowbar between the cutout and the floor and then wiggled it back and forth. *Crack*. The sound of cracking wood caused Carlita to cringe. "Please be careful with the floors."

"I'm tryin' Ma. I don't think this thing has been off in decades." Tony worked his way around the perimeter of the square and with each crack Carlita cringed, mentally counting the cost to have the damaged floor repaired.

Finally, the cracking ceased and Tony set the crowbar on the floor. "I think I got it loosened up." He rubbed his hands together before he reached for the metal ring a second time.

The splintered wood groaned in protest as Tony yanked on it several times before it finally gave way and the large piece of wood popped up. A plume of dust blasted upward and Carlita coughed.

Mercedes waved her hand in front of her face. "Good grief. Ah-ah achoo!"

"Bless you," Carlita said.

"I need the flashlight again," Tony said.

Carlita retrieved the flashlight that had rolled across the floor and handed it to Tony. He turned it on and shined the light into the large opening. "I see a ladder. Hang onto this." He handed the flashlight to his mother and scooted off the side.

Carlita beamed the light downward and watched as her son descended into the pitch-black abyss. "Be careful. No telling what's down there."

Tony's hand shot up causing Carlita to jump. "Oh my gosh. You scared me." She placed the flashlight in her son's outstretched hand.

"What do you see?" Carlita stuck her head in the opening as she peered over the side. The only thing visible was the light from the flashlight as it bobbed up and down on the dirt floor. It moved along the floor and then up the side of a brick wall.

The flashlight shifted and the light blinded Carlita. She clamped a hand over her eyes. "That's bright."

"Sorry." Tony lowered the flashlight. "You wanna come down here and check it out?"

"No," Carlita said.

"I do." Mercedes crawled to the edge of the opening. "Good thing I brought a second flashlight." She balanced the flashlight in one hand and grabbed the first rung of the ladder with her other. "Heave ho. Here we go."

Carlita watched her daughter scamper down the ladder.

When she reached the bottom, Mercedes looked up. "C'mon Chicken Little. There aren't any bodies."

"That we know of," Carlita replied as she reluctantly stuck her foot on the top rung. She descended the steps and with a little hop, landed on the uneven dirt floor. The ceiling was low and Carlita had to stoop forward to avoid hitting her head on the beams.

A dull fragment of light shone through the grimy basement window. With only a trickle of light, she could barely make out the layers of red bricks covering the walls.

Carlita shifted her gaze and spied some sort of doorway. She took a step closer. A thin layer of plaster covered the walls near the opening. The plaster had crumbled in several places, exposing a layer of cement underneath.

"Check this out," Carlita said.

Tony gingerly stepped over the rough floor as he made his way to the opening. He crept forward and then abruptly stopped.

Mercedes, who had been following close behind her brother, collided with him, stepping on the corner of his heel. "Ouch!"

"You shouldn't have stopped so suddenly," Mercedes said.

"I can't go any farther." He flashed his light onto the wall in front of him. "It's a dead end."

"Are you sure?" Mercedes slipped past her brother and ran her hand along what appeared to be the frame of a door. "Someone closed this off." She shifted her gaze and studied the overhead beams. "It looks like some sort of tunnel."

Mercedes squinted her eyes. "Is that what I think it is?" She let out an ear-piercing scream, "SPIDER!" and bolted from the tunnel. She didn't stop until she'd climbed the ladder and reached the safety of the upper level.

Tony stepped back inside the basement. "I wonder what's behind there."

Carlita squinted her eyes and studied the wall. "I heard Savannah is a maze of tunnels. We're so close to the river, I wonder if it leads to the Savannah River."

"Give me a couple sticks of dynamite and we'll find out," Tony said.

"You're kidding," Carlita said.

Tony shrugged. "Skip the dynamite. A jackhammer would work, too. I had a buddy who broke out of the big house by chipping away at a concrete wall."

"You don't say." Carlita eyed her son cautiously and then changed the subject. "I noticed some boxes stacked up in the corner. You mind taking a look to see what's inside?"

"Sure. Where are they?"

"Over here." Carlita led her son to the other side of the basement, to a pile of wooden crates.

Tony held his flashlight with one hand and reached for the top crate with his other. "There's some kinda marking on the outside." He shifted the light and studied the exterior. "I'll need to pry the cover off. Let's take them upstairs."

The box on the bottom was the heaviest and Tony struggled to carry it up the ladder.

Carlita carried the lightest of the three, the one on top.

Tony headed to the basement a second time to get the third box. After making sure there wasn't anything else down there, he climbed the ladder, slid the box to his mother and then eased the trap door into place.

Mercedes stood off to one side and watched. "Aren't you going to nail it down?"

"Nope. My plan is to blow a hole in the wall so we can find out what's on the other side."

"That's up for debate," Carlita said. Visions of her son blowing a hole in the bottom of her floor filled her head. "Let's figure out what's inside these boxes first."

Tony swiped at the thick layer of dust on the top of the box. "Stumping Dynamite." He reached for the crowbar. "Here goes nothing."

"Wait!" Mercedes lunged forward to stop her brother. "What if you blow us to smithereens?"

"I don't plan on it but you can stand somewhere else if it would make you feel safer." Tony tapped the top of the box with the tip of the crowbar. "Whatever is in here belongs to the property owner...Ma."

Mercedes and Carlita hurried to the other side of the room. "Be careful son," Carlita said.

"Here goes nothin'," Tony wedged the tip of the crowbar under the top of the box and began prying it open. Chunks of the cover broke off before he was finally able to remove it. "I don't see any explosives."

Mercedes and Carlita moved closer while Tony shifted the box so all three of them had a clear view. Inside was a large black bag. Tony pulled the bag out and shoved the box aside.

On closer inspection, Carlita noticed it was a drawstring bag.

Mercedes caught her mother's eye. "The bag looks awfully familiar."

Carlita's face turned an ashen color and she nodded. It reminded her of the small bag she and her daughter had found inside her deceased husband's safe deposit box. "It sure does."

Tony fumbled with the drawstrings and pulled them apart. He reached into the bag and pulled out a handful of precious gemstones.

Chapter 3

"Holy cannoli!" Tony shouted. "We hit the jackpot!" He handed the gems to his mother, reached his hand inside the bag a second time and pulled out another handful of gems. After the third handful, he tipped the bag over and emptied the contents onto the floor in front of them. "This is like winnin' the lottery!"

Tony scrambled across the floor to the second wooden box while Carlita scooped up the loose gems and dumped them back inside the black bag. She noticed several rusty old tools crammed in the bottom as she placed the bag back inside the box.

The second box contained a worn ledger, along with what appeared to be an antique cabinet. The cabinet was filled with a variety of old keys.

The third and final box contained another bag of precious gems. The bag was much smaller than the first. They also found a sliding ruler with a lever at the end as well as a tool with a round face. On the front of it was a scale with the numbers one through ten.

Tony picked up the tool with the round face and inspected it. "I'm not a gem man but I've seen this before. It's used to measure stones."

After double-checking to make sure the other two boxes were empty, the trio carefully placed the items back inside.

Tony stood. "We need to find a safe place to stash these 'til we figure out what we're gonna do with them."

Mercedes and Carlita each grabbed one of the lighter boxes while Tony carried the heavy box, the box with the gems and old tools, up the stairs to the apartment. "We gotta find out what's on the other side of the wall."

"I haven't decided what to do about that yet." Carlita stopped abruptly at the top of the stairs. A loud *THUNK* shook the floor.

"What in the world?" Mercedes jumped.

"You mean who in the world." Carlita's eyes narrowed as she stared at Elvira Cobb's apartment door. "Hard telling what the woman is doing now." A smaller, muffled *thunk* followed the first thunk.

Tony held the apartment door open and waited for his mother and sister to step inside the living room. "Is that one of your tenants making all that racket?"

"I think so and my guess is it's Elvira." Carlita set her box on the floor inside the door. "She's a royal pain in the rear. Somehow I managed to get one of the best tenants in the world and also one of the worst."

She explained to her son how Elvira had moved in not long ago. Since moving in, she'd attempted to stop them from opening the pawnshop using her position at the Savannah Architectural Society. She'd also tried to cut down one of the trees in the courtyard, succeeded in painting the outside of the building while working on an art project and nearly driven Carlita crazy.

The apartment lights flickered. A low buzzing sound followed the flicker. "I've had it!" Carlita clenched her fists. "I am going to find out what on earth that woman is doing inside her apartment. This is the third time today the lights have flickered."

Tony gazed at the flickering dining room light. "Something is sucking some major electrical juice."

Carlita flung the apartment door open, marched across the hall and pounded on Elvira's door. No one answered so Carlita tried again, pounding even louder. "Elvira! It's Carlita. I'd like to have a word with you."

Tony followed his mother into the hall and stood behind her. "Maybe it wasn't her."

"Oh it was!"

The door flew open and Elvira's plump figure filled the doorway. "Yes?"

"What is going on in there?" Carlita demanded. "It sounded like a cannon going off and we've been having brownouts all day."

"I don't know what you're talking about," Elvira said calmly. "I haven't noticed anything unusual." A small bright light flashed behind Elvira. It was followed by a loud buzzing sound.

"That! That noise." Carlita took a step forward. "I would like to take a look around your apartment."

"I don't know if I should let you in. Let me check my rental agreement." Elvira started to close the door and then caught a glimpse of Tony, still standing behind his mother.

The door shot back open. Elvira smoothed her gray hair. "My, my. Who is this tall drink of water?" She batted her eyes and tugged on the bottom of her stained t-shirt. "Tell me you're the new tenant moving across the hall."

Carlita shook her head. "This is my son, Tony. He's here for a visit and to help me get the pawnshop up and running."

"Oh." Elvira's face fell but she quickly recovered and the smile was back. "I guess it wouldn't hurt to let you have a quick look around." She snaked her arm around Carlita and grabbed hold of Tony's arm. "Would you like a tour? I'm a wonderful cook. English/Irish descent. I make a mean shepherd's pie."

Carlita remembered the dish Elvira had made the night they'd discovered a bat in her apartment. Her stomach churned as she remembered the disgusting smell. "We'll take your word for it." She hurried inside the apartment before Elvira could change her mind and stopped abruptly in the middle of the living room. "You painted the walls."

The walls of the apartment, which had been an off white, were now a kaleidoscope of colors. The wall that overlooked the courtyard was neon green. The opposite wall, what Carlita could see of it, was purple. "You painted the wall purple," she gasped.

"Magenta," Elvira corrected.

The kitchen walls were bright red. "And red," she said.

"Red is good for digestion," Elvira said. "The bedroom is orange." She turned to Tony and lowered her eyelids seductively. "Would you like to check it out?"

Despite her annoyance, Carlita chuckled under her breath and her son shot her a dark look as he took a step back. "I...no."

Another bolt of bright light flashed from the vicinity of the purple living room wall.

"Aha!" Carlita pointed at the wall of blinking bins. "It's coming from there." She walked to the other side of the room. "I noticed these bins last time I was in here and you never did tell me what all this stuff is." She waved her hands at the blinking lights.

"Computer equipment," Elvira said coolly. "I've scoured my lease with a fine tooth comb and nowhere does it say I can't have computer equipment."

The lights flickered again and the machines began to make a loud whirring noise.

"You're sucking too much juice," Carlita said. "What if you set this place on fire?"

"I wouldn't be surprised," Elvira sniffed. "This building has to be hundreds of years old. It's already a fire hazard."

Carlita took a menacing step toward her tenant.

Tony darted in front of his mother after noting the look in her eyes. He held up his hands. "Let me take a look at the breaker box. There may be a simple fix."

Carlita was livid and said the first thing that popped into her head. "If you burn this place down, I'm going to evict you."

Tony placed his hand under his mother's elbow and led her out of the apartment. "It's not worth it," he mumbled under his breath.

Elvira followed them into the outer hall. She ignored Carlita and turned to Tony. "Stop by later, luv. I'll have dinner waiting." She winked at Tony and shut her apartment door.

Carlita heard the deadbolt turn. She clenched her fists and her jaw tightened. "There are moments, way too many moments I want to strangle that woman with my bare hands."

"She can't be that bad," Tony said.

"You'll see," Carlita predicted. She strode back into her apartment.

Mercedes, who was sprawled out on the sofa watching television, grinned when she saw the look on her mother's face. "Another entertaining encounter with Elvira?"

Carlita flung herself into the recliner and closed her eyes. "One, two, three, four…"

"What are you doing?" Tony settled into the chair opposite his mother.

Mercedes snorted. "Elvira induced counting."

Carlita lifted her head and opened her eyes. "If you don't mind taking a look at the breaker box before Elvira follows through with her attempts to burn this place to the ground, I would be ever so grateful."

She told Tony where the electrical panel was located and then waited until he stepped out of the apartment and closed the door behind him. "Elvira invited Tony to dinner."

Mercedes burst out laughing. "You're kidding."

"Nope. She called him a tall drink of water, whatever that means."

"She thinks he's hot," Mercedes explained. "Poor Tony."

"Poor Tony? Poor *us*." Carlita changed the subject. "I'm hungry and don't feel like cooking. It's a nice night for a walk. Let's head down to the river. The last time Rambo and I walked down there, I discovered a new Italian restaurant I would like to check out."

"Sounds good." Mercedes hopped off the couch. She glanced at the door. "Are you going to tell Tony about the gems we found in Pops' safe deposit box?"

Carlita shrugged. "I guess so. I don't know what to think."

"I think Delmario, the man who originally owned this property, tried to pay Pops with some gems. Something happened and Delmario deeded this property to Pops. Pops, not wanting to move to Savannah, stuck the deeds, along with the bag of gems inside the safe deposit box."

"So the gems could be stolen." Carlita groaned. "What's next?"

"Hard telling," Mercedes said. She pointed to the boxes, stacked by the front door. "I'll do some research on them later."

Carlita didn't have time to answer. The power went out. Moments later, the power was back on and the lights in the living room beamed brighter.

Tony returned a short time later. "I think I fixed the problem."

"You murdered Elvira?" Carlita joked.

"Nah. I found the breaker box. There was a loose wire so I shut the power off and fixed it."

"So it might not have been Elvira's fault?"

"Not entirely, although it seems like she's sucking a lot of juice, which probably doesn't help," Tony said.

Carlita rose from the chair and hugged her son. "Thanks Tony. I appreciate you taking a look at it for me."

"I'll go get ready for dinner." Mercedes disappeared into her room and shut the door.

"I found a new Italian restaurant down by the water I'm dying to try," Carlita said. "I'd like to go check it out."

"I'm kinda beat after the long day," Tony said. "Do you mind if we just order pizza and hang out instead?"

"Of course not." Carlita smiled. "There's a New York style pizza place not far from here and they deliver."

Tony offered to take Rambo for a walk around the block while Carlita ordered the pizza. By the time he returned, the pizza had arrived.

Mercedes emerged from her room. "We're not going out for dinner, I take it."

"Tony said he was tired and asked if we could stay home instead." They settled in at the dining room table and discussed the basement and their "find." The trio unanimously agreed to keep mum about the content of the boxes until they had a chance to research what they'd found.

Carlita told Tony about the small bag of gems they'd found inside the safe deposit box, similar to the ones they found in the basement.

Tony grabbed a slice of pepperoni pizza and folded it in half. "So the gems in Pops' safe deposit box and the ones we found in the basement are linked."

"Yep." Mercedes nodded. "What if Delmario smuggled gems through the tunnel to the river? I think Delmario paid Pops with a bag of gems. Somewhere along the way, he deeded the properties to Pops."

"There's a chance your father was involved in a gem smuggling ring," Carlita said. "Which leads us to one major question…"

"Where did the gems come from?" Tony said.

Chapter 4

Whack! Whack! Whack! Carlita sat upright in bed. It took a moment for her to figure out what had woken her and then she heard it again. *Whack!*

"Elvira," Carlita gasped as she reached for her bathrobe. She flung her robe on and darted into the hall. Mercedes met her there. "What is that racket?"

"My first guess would be Elvira." Carlita jogged to the front door and yanked it open.

Whack! The sound wasn't coming from Elvira's apartment. It echoed from somewhere downstairs.

Carlita shifted her gaze to the empty sleeper sofa. "You don't think Tony is trying to tear out the basement wall?" She didn't wait for an answer as she raced down the steps.

The door leading to the pawnshop was ajar.

Whack!

Mercedes followed her mother down the steps and into the back room. "Yep. He's down there all right." She tiptoed to the opening in the floor and peered over the side. "Tony?"

There was a small noise and Tony appeared at the bottom of the ladder. "Yeah?"

"What are you doing?" Carlita shuffled next to her daughter and stared into the basement.

"I couldn't sleep so I figured I'd take a shot at busting through the wall."

"What if I don't want to know what's on the other side?" Carlita asked.

"I wanna know," Tony said. "I'm makin' some progress. By the time you get dressed, I should be through to the other side."

Carlita started to tell him to stop but it was too late. Tony and all of her sons were just like their father. Once they got something stuck in their head, there was no stopping them. "I'll go get dressed."

The women retraced their steps and made their way back inside the apartment. "I'll start the coffee," Carlita said. "I have a feeling this is going to be a very long day."

While the coffee brewed, she threw on a pair of old sweatpants and t-shirt, poured two to-go thermoses full of coffee and headed downstairs to check on her son.

"I got some coffee," she hollered down.

Tony took the thermoses from his mother and waited for her to climb down the ladder. He handed one of the thermoses to her before unscrewing the cap on his and taking a sip. "I got a big opening now. It's only a matter of time and we'll be able to see what's on the other side."

Carlita gazed warily at the hole. "I have a bad feeling about this."

"I got a good feeling about this." Tony sipped more coffee before he replaced the lid, set the thermos on the dirt floor and picked up his sledgehammer.

Carlita watched as he swung the sledgehammer and whacked the brick wall. Large chunks broke loose and landed on the other side. Tony lowered the sledgehammer and stuck his head in the opening. "Almost there."

He swung low and smashed the bottom layers of brick. "That oughta do the trick." Tony propped the sledgehammer against the concrete wall and reached for his flashlight. "Here goes nothin'."

He stepped over the pile of rubble and through the hole in the wall. "Agh!"

Carlita, startled by her son's scream, raced across the dirt floor. "Are you all right?"

"Yeah." Tony's head popped through the opening. "Just checkin' to make sure you're still out here in case I need you."

Carlita reached through the opening and slugged her son in the arm. "Don't scare me like that. You're gonna give me a heart attack."

"Hello?" Mercedes' voice echoed into the opening.

Carlita made her way over to the ladder. "We're down here dear." She shifted to the side and watched as her daughter descended the steps.

"I thought we were going to discuss knocking the wall down." Mercedes said when she reached the basement.

"I thought we were, too, but your brother had other ideas." Carlita pointed at the opening. "He's already busted through."

The women tiptoed over to the opening and Carlita peered into the darkness. "Did you find anything?"

"There's a tunnel," Tony said. "It kept goin' but the batteries in the flashlight were dying so I turned around and came back."

"I've got a heavy duty flashlight upstairs." Carlita hurried to the apartment.

Rambo was waiting by the door. He wagged his tail when she stepped inside. "I'll take you out in a few minutes. I'm sure Tony already took you out first thing, didn't he?"

Rambo let out a low moan and flopped down on the floor.

"I'll be back," she promised before she made her way to the hall closet to search for the flashlight. After checking to make sure that it worked, Carlita returned to the basement.

Tony took the flashlight from his mother and switched it on. "Much better."

Bright light beamed from the passageway and Carlita crept closer, peering over the top of the rubble. A musty smell permeated the air and she wrinkled her nose. "We won't have to worry about Elvira snooping around down here." Carlita's tenant claimed to have asthma and severe allergies as well as a sensitive nose.

Tony pointed the flashlight at the walls as he worked his way along the front part of the tunnel. "These walls are solid concrete. It looks like they covered them with some sort of plaster." He shifted closer. "I see something." He bent down and focused the light on a lower section of the wall. "Wonder what this is."

Carlita narrowed her eyes and stared at the section of wall where two long pieces of metal jutted out.

Tony grabbed one of the metal pieces and pulled. It swung out. He did the same thing with the other. "Never seen anything like this." He pushed the metal pieces back in place and started to stand when something caught Carlita's eye. "What's that?" She pointed at a section of the wall.

"What's what?"

"There. To the left of those metal brackets."

Tony shifted the light. He bent down a second time and studied the section before he reached out and brushed his fingers along the wall.

Small sections of the wall crumbled and fell to the floor. The moisture from the damp earth combined with the age of the walls had caused them to soften. "Better not wipe too hard," Carlita joked. "They might cave in on us."

"There's something here." Tony rubbed a little harder and another section of the wall, this one larger, gave way. He shined the light up and along the wall. "There's a cutout. Like someone added this section. See?"

Carlita followed the light. Her son was right. An uneven hairline crack formed a large square.

"Hand me the sledgehammer."

Mercedes grabbed the sledgehammer propped up against the wall and tossed it through the opening.

"Scaredy cat." Tony reached for the tool, took a step back and swung at the wall. His first swing broke through the flimsy exterior. He grabbed the flashlight and shined it inside the small hole. "There's something in there."

He swung at the wall a few more times, eventually creating a three-foot wide opening. Tony set the tool on the floor and shined the flashlight inside. "Oh no."

"Oh no?" Carlita repeated.

"It looks like there's a skull and a pile of bones inside."

Chapter 5

"That's not funny," Carlita gasped.

"I'm not joking," Tony said. "I'm dead serious…I mean, I'm serious."

Carlita momentarily forgot her fear and vaulted through the opening. "Where?" She leaned forward and stared into the opening. Sure enough, resting just inside the opening was a skull along with skeletal remains. She looked away and then glanced at the remains a second time. "It looks like they've been here awhile."

Mercedes followed her mother through the opening and peered over her shoulder. "This is probably the person who has been haunting the upstairs. They wanted us to find their body."

Carlita shivered. "You need to stop watching horror flicks, Mercedes." She turned to her son. "Don't touch anything. We need to call the cops."

"Wait!" Mercedes reached into her back pocket and pulled out her cell phone. She took several pictures of the inside of the opening, the opening itself and then backed up as she took a picture of the corridor. "These might come in handy."

Mercedes and Carlita made their way into the basement and climbed the ladder to the upper floor.

Tony placed the sledgehammer and flashlight on the floor by the door and followed the women up the ladder. "You do know an investigation will delay the opening of the pawnshop."

"It can't be helped," Carlita said as they climbed the stairs to their apartment. "I'll call the Savannah-Burnham Police Department." She stepped inside and grabbed her cell phone off the kitchen counter.

"I have their number." Mercedes switched her cell phone on and rattled off the number while her mother dialed.

"You got the police department on speed dial?" Tony asked.

"Mercedes went in for a job interview not long ago," Carlita whispered. "Hello? Yes. This is Carlita Garlucci. I live at 210 Mulberry Street. My children and I were cleaning out our basement and well, we found what we think are human skeletal remains and they've been there awhile."

"Why do you wanna work for the fuzz?" Tony asked his sister in a low voice.

Carlita waved at him to shush and pointed to the phone. "Okay. I'll meet them in the back alley." She disconnected the line. "They're on the way." She stepped into the hall and headed down the stairs.

Carlita's other tenant, Shelby Towns and her daughter, Violet, were on their way up. Shelby was juggling several bags of groceries. "Hello Mrs. Garlucci…Carlita." Shelby smiled.

"I got candy." Violet held out a small sucker so Carlita could see.

"Your sucker looks yummy." Carlita grinned.

"It's purple berry," Violet told her.

"It's cherry," her mother laughed.

"Where's Rambo?" Violet asked.

"Rambo is inside. I have to meet someone outdoors but if you're going to be home later, I'll bring him over for a visit." She gazed at Shelby who nodded. "Yep. We're in for the rest of the day. We're going to pop some popcorn and watch the *Little Mermaid* movie later."

"Sounds like fun. I'll bring my son, Tony, by to meet you. He's in town for a visit but we're hoping he's going to make it permanent."

They said their good-byes, with Carlita promising to stop by around seven o'clock before she headed out the back door and into the alley to wait for the police to arrive.

Mercedes joined her a few minutes later. "Do you think the remains have anything to do with the previous owners, George and Louise Delmario?"

"I don't know what to think. Until the police can identify the remains or at least tell us how long the remains have been hidden behind the wall, it's hard to tell." Carlita shook her head. "I don't even know how long the Delmarios owned this place."

A police car pulled into the alley moments later, followed by a crime scene van. Two officers and two crime scene investigators met her near the door. Carlita led them into the shop and down the ladder to the basement.

She waited near the side and pointed toward the opening. "The person is in there, on the right hand side. You'll need a flashlight."

The officers and the crime scene investigators disappeared through the opening and then reappeared moments later. One of the investigators exited the basement and returned a short time later carrying a large bag. He and the other investigator headed back inside the tunnel while the two police officers watched.

"We'd like to ask you a few questions, Mrs. Garlucci," one of the officers told her.

"We can do that upstairs where it's a little less claustrophobic." She led the way up the ladder and into the hall connecting the store to the rear entrance.

The second officer pulled a notepad and pen from the folder he was carrying. "Start from the beginning."

Carlita explained how the previous day she and her children had been going over their plans to open the pawnshop and Tony had discovered a trap door inside the kitchen cupboard. She told the officers how they had removed the cabinet, found the door, pried it open and made their way into the basement.

"So you've never been in your basement before yesterday?" The officer stopped writing.

"No. The building was recently renovated and my construction supervisor, Bob Lowman, said he thought that perhaps the entrance to the basement might be in one of the other buildings. We had no idea it was under the cabinet."

"Huh." The cop paused as he studied her face. "Interesting."

Carlita continued. "We noticed there was some sort of tunnel that had been sealed and my son decided to find out where it went so he knocked a hole in the wall this morning."

"And how did you find the body?" the second officer asked.

"The tunnel wall looked different, like there was some sort of cutout someone had walled up. Tony, my son, tapped on the outside. It sounded hollow so he took a sledgehammer and knocked a hole in it. That's when we found the skeletal remains inside."

She didn't mention the wooden boxes since she wasn't sure she needed to tell them about the gems. They were on her property, but then, so was the body, unless the tunnel belonged to someone else. They didn't ask. She didn't offer.

The officers thanked her for her time and told her they would stop by her apartment before they left.

Carlita stepped into the hall and ran smack dab into Elvira Cobb. "What's up with the cops?"

"It's a long story," Carlita said.

Elvira lifted a brow. "I have time."

Carlita sucked in a breath and closed her eyes. "We found skeletal remains in a tunnel connected to our basement."

Elvira's eyes lit up. "Can I see?"

"No. The investigators are down there as well as the police. Besides, the basement is full of mold and mildew. You'd have an allergic reaction for sure."

"Not anymore. I bought these special face masks to filter the air," Elvira said. She rubbed her hands together. "Maybe later, after the cops leave, you can show me what you found."

The last thing Carlita wanted was to show Elvira the basement, the body or the tunnel. "I'm sure they won't allow us to go down there."

"I suppose," Elvira said. "Well, I better get going. I have a few errands to run." She turned to go then swung back. "Say, I'm having a small problem with my plumbing. Can that gorgeous son of yours stop by later to take a look at it for me?"

The warning bells went off in Carlita's head. "I think I should take a look at it first." She waited until Elvira exited the building before trudging up the stairs. "Problem with your plumbing my foot."

She stepped into the apartment and caught a glimpse of Tony and Rambo out on the deck. Carlita opened the slider and made her way outside.

"I see the cops are still here."

Carlita flopped into one of the chairs and rolled her eyes. "Yeah. They asked a few questions and told me they'd let me know the status before they left."

"Did you tell them about the…" Tony's voice trailed off.

"Nope." Carlita shook her head. "They didn't ask and I didn't tell."

"Technically, it's none of their business," Tony said. "Those boxes were on your property. They may not have anything to do with the body."

Carlita nodded, but in the back of her mind, she thought just the opposite. Somehow, the gems and the body were linked, but how? She changed the subject. "Any word from your brother, Vinnie?"

"Nah." Tony shook his head. "He'll surface eventually."

"Hopefully not floating face down in the Hudson River," she grimaced. "I wish he would at least call me."

"There's a reason he's not," Tony said.

A knot formed in the pit of Carlita's stomach and she whispered a small prayer for her oldest son.

She sat there for several long moments in deep thought as she watched the investigators remove items from their van and carry them inside.

"This isn't helping." Determined to take her mind off her son's disappearance and the body, she stood. "Let's go for a walk, down by the river."

Rambo's ears perked up and he scrambled to his feet. "You know what I'm saying, don't you Rambo?"

They stepped inside and Carlita grabbed her house keys then made her way into the hall. She knocked on Mercedes' bedroom door.

The door flew open and Carlita jumped back as she clutched her chest. "I swear. As long as I live I will never get used to you opening the door like that."

"Sorry Mom. What's up?"

"Tony, Rambo and I are going for a walk over by the river and Morrell Park. You wanna go with us?"

"Nah." Mercedes' eyes slid to the side. "I'm working on a project."

"Okay. We'll be back." The door closed and Carlita stared at it for a moment. She'd stumbled upon a draft of a book her daughter had been writing, *Murder, Mayhem and the Mafia*. A

Mob Daughter's Confessions. So far, Mercedes hadn't mentioned the book to her mother.

Carlita hoped someday her daughter would tell her. Until then, she decided to keep the fact she'd read the first few lines of the draft to herself.

Tony, Rambo and Carlita headed down the steps. "Wait here." Carlita made her way to the trap door. "Hello?"

One of the officers, covered in a layer of dirt, came into view. "Yes?"

"My son and I are taking our dog for a walk down by the river," she said.

"We'll be here for a little while longer," the officer said. "Stop by when you get back."

Carlita promised she would and then headed outside where Tony and Rambo waited. "How they doin'?" Tony asked.

"I didn't ask. One of the cops is covered in a layer of dirt," she said. "Hopefully they'll do what they need to do today and won't need to come back."

"I hope so too," Tony agreed.

As they walked, Carlita pointed out the other businesses in Walton Square - A Scoop in Time Ice Cream Shop, Shades of Ink Tattoo Shop and Riverfront Real Estate.

"What about this place?" Tony pointed to the sign in the window of what had once been Walton Square Souvenirs. "Maybe you should buy it."

Carlita shook her head. "I have my hands full as it is. Annie, the woman who owns Riverfront Real Estate, heard through the grapevine the place is under contract."

She went on. "Annie told me the building was originally a single family home and the descendants of the original owners are purchasing the property with plans to renovate it and turn it into a bed and breakfast."

Carlita took a step back and inspected the exterior of the multi-story structure. "With some sprucing up, this would be a beautiful home." They continued past the vacant building and the real estate office.

When they reached the end of the block, they crossed the busy street. Tony stopped abruptly. "Check that out Ma."

A man dressed in pirate garb and carrying a fake sword stood on a small porch talking to a group of people wearing bright yellow tour stickers.

Perched on the pirate's shoulder was a parrot. "And then I told 'em it was time ta walk the plank."

Tony and Carlita inched closer to the outer edges of the group to listen. The man talked of buried treasure and pirate ships. When he mentioned secret passageways under the city, Carlita nudged Tony. "I wonder if the tunnel we found under our building leads all the way to the river."

Chapter 6

Mother and son waited until the tourists moved on. The pirate turned to go.

Carlita lifted her gaze to read the sign on the porch, *'The Parrot House.'* "Wait!"

The pirate spun around. "Yes?"

"We own property over on Mulberry Street. My son discovered a tunnel underneath our building."

"Ah." The pirate nodded and the patch on his eye shifted. "Yur not far from here."

He answered the question before Carlita could even ask.

"There be a maze of tunnels under the city, some of them blocked off over the years, but I be bettin' your tunnel eventually connects to the Parrot House." He waved them onto the porch.

"My name's Pirate Pete." The man extended his hand and lowered his voice. "Pete Taylor, owner of the Parrot House. This here is Gunner. He likes to make the sound of a machine gun." To prove the point, Gunner began chattering. *Tak-tak-tak-tak.*

"Gunner loves sunflower seeds." Pete reached into his pocket, pulled out a fist full of seeds and dumped them in Carlita's hand.

She held out her hand. Gunner bobbed forward and nibbled the seeds.

Rambo barked, which scared Gunner and he hopped onto Pete's back.

"Rambo. Don't do that," Carlita said. She turned to Pete. "I'm sorry."

"No worries," Pete said. "Would you like to take a look at me tunnel?"

"No," Carlita said.

"Yes," Tony said.

"I guess." Carlita looped Rambo's leash around one of the stair rails and followed her son and Pete inside. "Do you think Rambo will be okay out here?"

"I'll have Sue, our hostess, keep an eye on him," Pete said. He led them through the front door of the Parrot House Restaurant. "Sue, can you please keep an eye on the dog tied up out front? We'll be back in a minute."

"Of course." Sue smiled at Carlita and Tony, and then shifted her gaze to the front porch and Rambo.

Pete, accompanied by Tony and Carlita, passed by a grand staircase and through a cozy dining area where servers waited on tables. They zigzagged past a second, larger eating area, a modern state-of-the-art kitchen and a set of swinging doors, which led to a separate storage area.

It reminded Carlita of the spot where their trap door was located. "This looks familiar."

Pete placed Gunner inside his birdcage and the parrot promptly hopped up on his perch. "Stay away from me buried treasure."

Pete laughed. "Gunner thinks he's a pirate."

"Watch out for the pirates!" Gunner squawked. "They'll steal your booty."

Pete bent down as he reached for a square handle. He tugged on the handle, lifted the cover and flipped it over. "We cleaned up down here a couple years back after the kitchen flooded. We don't use it for much these days. It's too damp. That and the fact it connects to other tunnels."

"I see." Carlita nodded.

Pete made his way down the cement steps. Tony followed him and Carlita brought up the rear. The basement area looked almost identical to their basement. The smell, the size, the small windows. "This looks like ours."

The only difference was there was a wide opening leading from the basement to the corridor. "Have you explored the tunnels?"

Pete nodded. "Some of 'em. It ain't for the faint of heart. There be lots of spiders. Not right here, but in other areas, there's even some mattresses and clothing."

Carlita wrinkled her nose. "People live in the tunnels?"

"Yep. Homeless is my guess. You can access parts of the tunnel from the street. Like I said, it ain't safe." He shrugged. "Over the years business owners started sealing off the entrances to their properties to keep out the riff raff."

"And we just blew ours wide open," Carlita said. She eyed her son, who shrugged.

"As soon as I have a chance to check it out and the cops leave, I'll seal it off again," Tony promised.

"Cops?" Pirate Pete eyed them.

"We uh…" Carlita's voice trailed off.

"Found a body in the hallway. Somebody hollowed out a section of the tunnel wall, dumped a body inside and then covered it up."

"I'd be sayin' I was surprised, but I'm not." Pete shook his head. "These tunnels are a haven for criminals. Any idea who it is?"

"Not yet," Tony said. "The police are still investigating."

They followed Pete down the hallway a short distance. He stopped and pointed at burn marks in the wooden ceiling, which was part of the Parrot House's floor. "We found these burn marks a couple months ago. Someone was trying to torch the place. Just my suggestion, but I'd be securin' my basement if I were you." They began to retrace their steps and Carlita studied the floor as she walked.

She noticed a set of metal bars, similar to the ones Tony had found, jutting out of the wall. Carlita stopped and pointed at the bars. "We found a set of these near the entrance to our tunnel. Do you know what they are?"

"Yes ma'am," Pete said. He knelt down and extended the bars. "Back in the day, there was no such thing as funeral homes or morgues. Property owners would place a long board on top of these two bars and then they would bring dead bodies down here for storage until the hearse came to pick them up to take them to the cemetery for burial."

Carlita shivered involuntarily. "I'm sorry I asked."

They ascended the steps and waited while Pirate Pete replaced the trap door and secured the lock. He wiped the palms of his hands on his striped buccaneer pants before checking his watch. "I got to get goin'. I got another group of tourists headed my way."

They followed Pete to the front porch and thanked him for his time. Carlita started down the steps.

"Hey!"

Carlita stopped and turned back.

"I heard someone bought the old Alder-Delaney place and plan to turn it into a bed and breakfast. That'll give the Cobblestone B&B a run for their money."

"I heard the same thing," Carlita said. "Do you know the house's history?"

"Oh yeah," Pete said. "The place is reportedly haunted. The original owner, James Alder, moved here from England. He was a sea merchant by trade. Rumor has it he murdered his first and second wives and inherited a small fortune."

Ding. Ding. The trolley rumbled down the brick street. "Heard Alder died in the old house. Took weeks to find his body after someone in the neighborhood began to smell something funny and the police investigated."

The trolley shuddered to a stop. Carlita thanked Pirate Pete for his time and for showing them his basement before Tony and she continued down the sidewalk with Rambo in tow.

They crossed the street and walked to the park. It was a beautiful afternoon and the perfect weather for a leisurely stroll.

Rambo attempted to chase after a bunny rabbit that hopped across the manicured grass and Tony held tight. "I know you're itchin' to close up the tunnel and I can't say as I blame you, but first I'm gonna do a little more exploration, just as soon as the investigators give us the all clear."

"Speaking of which, we should head back," Carlita said. They finished their walk and made their way back to the apartment. The crime scene investigators and their van were gone. The police car was still parked in the alley and the two officers, the first to arrive on the scene, stood in the alley talking to Elvira and Mercedes.

"...and we may be back tomorrow, depending on whether the teams of investigators are able to determine the cause of death," one of the officers said.

Carlita hurried over. "Whoever was inside the wall has been there for a very long time."

The officer half turned. "Yes ma'am. Mrs. Garlucci. I was telling your daughter there is a maze of tunnels under the city and anyone who knows where to look can access parts of the tunnel from the streets. In other words, you may want to block access once our investigators wrap up the investigation."

"I couldn't agree more." Carlita nodded. "I just met Pirate Pete Taylor. Pete owns the Parrot House Restaurant and he told my son and me the same thing."

After the officers left, Carlita turned to the trio. "Under no circumstances is anyone," she spun around and faced her son, "including you, allowed to go inside the tunnel. It's dangerous."

Tony nodded.

Elvira snorted.

Carlita wagged her finger at her tenant and Elvira pretended not to see it.

Mercedes' eyes grew round as saucers. "This whole place is haunted. I thought it was because this used to be a casket company but now I wonder if it may be the ghost of whoever is buried in the basement, roaming around, searching for justice."

"Justice, schmustice." Tony waved his hand. "I don't believe in no boogeyman."

Elvira stepped inside the building. "Historic Savannah as a whole has a lot of paranormal activity. I wouldn't be surprised if this place has an unhappy spirit hanging around. Why just the other night, I was saying to myself, 'Elvira, the clanking and rattling you hear coming from the register ducts might be a spirit roaming around this old place.'"

She reached for the handrail and started up the stairs. "I would think a tenant who is willing to live in a haunted dwelling should get some sort of break on their rent."

"You could always move out," Carlita interrupted. "I'd be happy to terminate your lease."

Elvira stopped abruptly. "It was just a thought. I'm quite content in my little abode. No sense in jumping the gun." She resumed her stair climb and stopped when she reached the upper hall. "I believe a little digging around into the backgrounds and history of the owners, past and previous, is in order."

Carlita wasn't sure if Elvira was threatening her but she didn't take kindly to the comment. "Maybe you'll find out we're mass murderers, waiting to pounce on our next victim." She grinned evilly at Elvira, who shrank back.

"I was kidding." Elvira hurried to her apartment door, swung the door open and disappeared inside.

"I don't think it will help," Mercedes said.

"Me either," Carlita replied. "That woman is the most aggravating, annoying, irritating and nosy woman I have ever met."

"So why'dja let her move in?" Tony asked.

Carlita rolled her eyes. "It's a long story." She glanced warily at Elvira's door. "Somehow, I have a feeling this is not the end of the matter. I saw the glint in Elvira's eyes. She's dying to snoop around in our basement."

She shrugged her shoulders and reached for the doorknob. "Of course, I could be wrong. She's just so unpredictable."

If only Carlita knew.

Chapter 7

When Carlita found out Tony was on his way to visit, she'd purchased all the ingredients to whip up one of her middle son's favorite dishes.

Carlita slipped her apron on before pulling her grandmother's family recipe box from the cabinet. She flipped through the recipes until she found the one for bowtie pasta with Italian sausage.

She'd made the bowtie pasta ahead of time and pulled the packet of frozen pasta from the freezer to thaw. Next, she removed the package of spicy Italian sausage from the refrigerator, placed it in a frying pan and began cooking the meat. After the meat was partially cooked, she added diced onions and minced garlic.

When the meat, along with the spices, finished cooking, she drained it, set it aside and headed to the tomato plants on her deck where she pulled six ripe red tomatoes from the vine. Back inside the kitchen, she made quick work of chopping the fresh tomatoes.

She added the tomatoes, some heavy cream, salt and her special blend of Italian seasoning to the pan. She eased the pan back onto the burner and turned the heat to medium to simmer.

While the sauce thickened, she placed the package of bowtie pasta in a bowl of warm water.

"Something smells delicious." Tony walked into the kitchen and peered over his mother's shoulder, sniffing appreciatively. "You made my favorite dish."

"I did." Carlita nodded. "Grab the salad from the fridge and set the table while I finish mixing this together."

Mercedes wandered in to help. "How come you only make the good stuff when we have company?"

"Because we can't eat all these big family-style dishes ourselves, Mercedes. Besides, I have to make something to tempt your brothers to come visit," she joked.

She mixed the pasta and sauce together, and then dumped it into a large serving bowl before carrying it to the dining room table.

Mercedes set the napkins and silverware in the center of the table and pulled out a chair. "While you were making dinner, I decided to do a little research on the history of this place. After the casket company went out of business, a guy by the name of Smythe bought it. He's the one who turned the upstairs into apartments."

Carlita reached for her fork. "What did he do with the downstairs?"

"He opened a supply store for merchants. They sold a little of everything…lanterns, rope, dried meats…items sailors and ships captains could use on board a ship. They even carried some medicinal items."

Carlita stabbed her lettuce with her fork and chewed thoughtfully. "It makes sense. This would be the perfect location for a store since we're not far from the river."

Mercedes nodded. "Yellow fever was on the rise and it appeared Mr. Smythe was selling a concoction he claimed cured it." She scooped a fork full of pasta and took a big bite.

"I remember during the trolley tour we took the guide told us yellow fever killed thousands of Savannah residents," Carlita said.

"Yep." Mercedes nodded.

Tony reached for a slice of crusty bread. "Maybe someone died of yellow fever and this Smythe fellow hid the body behind the wall."

"But why?" Carlita asked. "So many people died of yellow fever. There would be no reason for Smythe to try to hide a body."

"I think the body has something to do with the gems we found in the basement," Carlita said.

She thought about the pouch of gems she'd discovered in the safe deposit box and Delmario's mysterious death. "Remember George Delmario's murder was never solved."

She continued. "If the investigators can pinpoint the length of time the skeletal remains were sealed behind the wall, we'll have a better idea of who owned this place during that time period."

The subject moved to the tunnels under the City of Savannah. Tony scraped the last of his pasta off the plate. "I promise to seal the tunnel, but first I think we should check it out. There may be something we're missing and unless we look, we'll never know for sure."

"I…"

Tony lifted a hand. "Ma, I promise after one more look around I'll seal it shut."

"I like the idea of the wrought iron gate," Carlita said. "Brick would be cheaper and equally as effective I suppose."

"Done," Tony said. "As soon as the investigators wrap up their investigation, I'll check it out."

"There's one more thing," Mercedes said. "According to several articles I read, there was a gem smuggling ring in this area. In fact, one story reported there was a large shipment of gems that mysteriously vanished from a cargo ship near the river. They never found the gems, valued at hundreds of thousands of dollars."

Carlita cast an uneasy glance at the box near the door. "I think I know where some of them ended up."

The trio made quick work of clearing the table and cleaning the kitchen. "I told Shelby we would stop by today so you could meet her."

"Who is Shelby?"

"The new neighbor across the hall," Mercedes said. "She has the most adorable little girl, Violet. Violet loves Rambo."

"Yes, she does." Carlita smiled. "Shelby was in a tough spot so we let her move in at a reduced monthly rent rate." She explained to her son how the poor young mother had been living in a shelter for homeless women. She'd gotten a part-time job at the post office but with no car, Shelby needed to live close to downtown so she could walk to Violet's babysitter as well as work.

"You got a heart of gold." Tony kissed his mother's cheek. "But being nice don't pay the bills."

"True," Carlita agreed, "but I would hope if any of my children was in a similar situation, someone would do the same for one of you."

"Yeah, I guess you're right," Tony agreed.

"Let's run over there before it gets too late." Carlita headed for the door and then stopped. "I almost forgot that I want to share some of our leftovers." She darted into the kitchen, grabbed the plastic storage container she'd filled with pasta and met her children in the hall.

Carlita led the way across the hall to Shelby's front door and tapped lightly. The door opened a crack. "Hello Carlita." The petite brunette swung the door open. "Violet was just asking if Rambo was coming for a visit."

"Shoot! I forgot to bring Rambo."

"I'll get him." Tony strode across the hall and disappeared into their apartment, returning moments later with Rambo.

Violet darted into the hall and wrapped her arms around Rambo's neck. "I've been waiting *all* day to see you." The young child led Rambo into the apartment and to her bedroom in the back.

"Come in." Shelby waved them inside. "Well? What do you think?"

Carlita glanced around the cozy apartment. When Mercedes and she had discovered that, other than the women's shelter donating beds to sleep in and a few cooking utensils, Shelby and her daughter didn't have a stick of furniture, they had gone to a local secondhand furniture store and purchased living room furniture and a dining room table for the small family.

"It looks like a home," Carlita said, nodding her head in approval.

"Thanks to you," Shelby said.

"Oh! Before I forget." Carlita handed the container of leftovers to Shelby. "I made a bowtie pasta dish for dinner and had a ton of leftovers."

"Thank you. You shouldn't have." Shelby took the dish and gave Tony, who stood next to his mother, a nervous glance.

"Where are my manners?" Carlita grasped Tony's arm. "Shelby, this is my son, Tony. He's here to help us set up shop downstairs."

Shelby extended a hand. "A pleasure to meet you."

Tony took her hand. "Same here. I'm pretty good at do-it-yourself-projects. If you need anything while I'm here, just holler."

"I'll do that," Shelby said softly. She tucked a stray strand of hair behind her ear, a shy smile warming her face.

Violet and Rambo raced into the living room. "When do we get popcorn and a movie?" she asked her mom and then turned to Carlita. "Can Rambo eat popcorn?"

Carlita bent down so she was eye level with the young girl. "I'm sorry Violet. We can't stay to watch your movie. It's almost Rambo's bedtime." She winked at Shelby. "But we'll be back to visit again soon," she promised.

Violet's face fell. "Okay." She quickly brightened. "My daddy is coming over later."

"He is?" Carlita cast Shelby a glance. The young mother's eyes widened. She gave a small shake of her head and reached for her daughter's hand. "Let's walk Rambo back home."

"Okay. C'mon Rambo." Violet led the way into the hall.

Shelby brought up the rear. "I noticed police cars in the alley earlier today. Is everything all right?"

"Yes. We uh…" Carlita didn't know where to start. She didn't want to scare the young mother half to death.

"We found skeletal remains in a tunnel in the basement," Mercedes blurted out. "But they look real old so we think they've been there awhile."

"Oh no." Shelby frowned.

Carlita patted her shoulder. "We'll let you know if it's anything worth worrying about," she assured her.

"I heard there are mazes of tunnels under Savannah," Shelby said.

"So it seems," Carlita murmured. She leaned over and gave Violet a gentle hug. "Be a good girl for Mommy."

"I will." Violet solemnly promised.

"Thanks again for the food," Shelby said. "For everything."

"You're welcome dear." Carlita hugged Shelby.

She turned to Tony. "It was nice to meet you." Shelby smiled. "Thanks for offering to help me."

The trio waited until Shelby and Violet disappeared inside their apartment before heading inside theirs.

Tony strolled to the living room sofa and flopped down. He leaned back and placed his hands behind his head. "So what's Shelby's story? She married?"

"Violet and Shelby lived in a shelter and had little more than the clothes on their backs when they moved in. Mercedes did a little digging and found out Shelby is married. Her husband's name is Robert but I've never seen a man around."

Carlita continued. "We labeled the doorbells downstairs with each tenant's name and Shelby asked us to remove hers."

"She's hiding from someone," Tony said.

"That would be my guess," Carlita nodded. She lifted her hands over her head and yawned. "We need to take Rambo out for a few minutes and then I'm ready to turn in for the night."

"I have a little project to wrap up," Mercedes said. "You two go on ahead." She disappeared into her room while Tony and Carlita headed downstairs to walk Rambo and check on the courtyard.

When they reached the bottom of the stairs, Carlita noticed the door leading to the pawnshop was ajar. "I'm positive I shut the door." She nudged the door open and stuck her head inside.

A dim flash of light flickered. "I know we locked this place up earlier."

"Let me go first Ma." Tony eased past his mother, pushed the door open and stepped into the storage room. "Someone is in the basement."

Chapter 8

One word, one person came to mind. "Elvira!" Carlita groaned. She hurried behind Tony as they stepped close to the open trap door. A flash of light beamed up.

"Elvira!" Carlita shouted.

Tony held a finger to his lips. "What if it's not Elvira? Let me get my gun."

"Go right ahead but I'll bet a million bucks it's my pain in the rear tenant." She waited while Tony headed back to the apartment, returning a short time later, gun in hand.

"I'll go first." Tony descended the ladder. Carlita followed him down.

A battery-operated lantern sat in one corner. In another corner was a flashlight propped up against the wall, the light beaming onto the ceiling.

"Hello?" Tony tightened his grip on the gun and took a step toward the tunnel. "Who's there?"

Carlita stayed close behind Tony as they crept into the tunnel. Up ahead, she could see another, smaller light as it bobbed up and down. The light grew brighter and the sound of footsteps grew louder.

A dark figure came into view. "Elvira Cobb!" Carlita shouted. "What in the world do you think you're doing?" She stared at her tenant, dressed from head to toe in black. Hanging around Elvira's neck was a respirator. She was wearing a headband. Attached to the front of the headband was a light.

"Good grief! What's that?"

"This?" Elvira reached up and pulled the headband off. "It's my version of a miner's headlamp. Check it out." She handed it to Carlita.

Carlita stared at the stretchy headband. "I swear I've seen it all now."

"I can never get those darned plastic ones to stay on my head so I made my own."

"I'd like to say I'm surprised but I'm not." Carlita handed the headband back. "This place is off limits. The investigators told us to stay out of here. Not only that, I told you to stay away from here."

"I thought I overheard you say you were gonna seal it off and I was dying to see what was down here. There are mazes of tunnels in Savannah. Did you know this one forks off?" Elvira rattled on. "I think one of these tunnels leads to the Parrot House. The other one might even lead to the river."

Tony interrupted. "Did you see anything?"

"Nah. I heard Carlita screeching at me so I turned around and came back."

Tony glanced at his mother. "We're already here. Why don't we scope it out?"

Carlita was on the fence. On the one hand, the entire tunnel and Pirate Pete's warning that vagrants were camping out in the tunnels caused her to pause. On the other hand, she wanted to put the whole tunnel, treasure and digging up bodies to rest.

Despite the nagging feeling that something bad was about to happen, she relented. "Okay. Just this once, but after tonight and the investigators give us the all clear, we're sealing this baby off."

Carlita retraced her steps and picked up the lantern and flashlight. She handed the flashlight to her son while Elvira strapped her makeshift miner's headlamp onto her head.

"I'll lead the way." Tony stepped in front of Elvira and Carlita brought up the rear. A tickle ran down her arm and Carlita slapped at her elbow.

"What was that noise?" Tony stopped abruptly.

"I hit myself," Carlita said. "It feels like there's something crawling on me."

"I hope it's not a brown recluse." Elvira shifted her headlamp and studied the wall. "I saw a couple earlier. I'd steer clear of the walls. They won't bother you if you don't bother them."

They continued walking and stopped when they got to the spot where the tunnel branched off. Elvira turned her head and her high beam "head light" illuminated the corridor to the left. "We should try this way first."

As they walked, Carlita studied the walls and ceiling, more in an attempt to keep an eye out for creepy crawly creatures than to explore. The tunnel ended abruptly when they hit another brick wall. "It's the end of the road, uh, tunnel."

The trio backtracked, passing by the section of tunnel that led to their property. The tunnel made several sharp turns before it, too, ended abruptly, blocked by a wrought iron gate.

"This was a bust," Tony said. He flashed his light around the perimeter of the gate.

"Another dead end," Carlita said. She took a step closer and shined her flashlight around the frame of the door. "This gate doesn't go all the way to the top. There's a gap."

She shifted her light and beamed it down the corridor and onto a rusty ladder, similar to the one in her basement.

"So close and yet so far," Elvira said. "Might as well head back."

The trio trudged back through the tunnel and stopped when they reached the basement.

Carlita snapped her fingers. "I've got an idea! What time is it?"

Tony glanced at his watch. "Eight forty-five. Why?"

"There's someone who may be able to help us out but it's too late to do anything tonight," Carlita said. "It will have to wait until tomorrow, after the investigators leave." She hurried up the ladder, across the hall and into the apartment.

Carlita grabbed her cell phone and joined Tony and Elvira in the hall moments later. She looked up from her phone. "Are you sure you left everything the way the investigators had it? If they find out we were snooping around they're not going to be happy."

Tony gave his mother a thumbs up. "It was like we were never even there."

"Good." Carlita shifted her gaze to her phone as she scrolled the screen. When she found Annie Downton's name, she typed a quick text. "Hi Annie. I have a favor to ask. Would you and Tinker be available to help us with a little intel tomorrow?"

She hit send and lowered the phone.

Tony pointed at the phone. "Who was that?"

"Annie Downton. She owns the real estate office across the street. Annie has a cool gizmo. It might be perfect to help us get past the gate and find out what's on the other side."

Annie texted back. "Sure. I have a meeting with a potential client at 9:00 a.m. but I am free afterward."

"Great," Carlita replied. "I'll be over at ten to explain." She pressed send and turned her phone off. "If the investigators wrap things up tomorrow, Annie and Tinker may be able to help us out."

"Who is Tinker?" Tony and Elvira asked in unison.

"You'll see." Carlita smiled.

***

Carlita tossed and turned all night, certain a creepy crawly venomous spider had hitched a ride upstairs and was now in bed with her. She switched the light on several times but each time she checked, there was nothing.

Finally, in the early morning light, she crept out of bed and into the hall. Rambo, who had bunked with Tony on the sleeper sofa, met her at the door.

She patted his head. "Let me throw some clothes on and I'll take you for an early morning walk," she whispered before heading to the bathroom. She emerged a short time later and Rambo and she headed down the stairs.

Carlita had recently cleared a parking area at the end of the alley and off to one side for both her vehicle and her tenants' vehicles. She had left a small grassy area for Rambo and he trotted ahead. After he inspected the vehicles parked in the lot, he wandered around the perimeter of the grassy area before taking care of business.

Fall was right around the corner. Although the late afternoons were still warm, the mornings were cool, almost crisp. It reminded Carlita of New York.

Rambo and Carlita walked around the entire block before heading home. When they reached the upper hall that connected the apartments, Carlita noticed a small ray of light beaming out from under Elvira's apartment door. She shook her head. "I swear the woman never sleeps."

She quietly let herself into the apartment and waited for Rambo to step inside before closing the door and turning the lock.

"I wondered where you snuck off to." Tony's deep voice caused Carlita to jump.

She clutched her chest and spun around. "Oh my gosh! You're going to give me a heart attack. Your sister does the same thing."

"Sorry Ma. Rambo woke me up when he jumped off the bed."

Carlita turned the floor lamp on and made her way into the kitchen. "I'll make some coffee."

Tony headed to the bathroom while Carlita began working on a makeshift breakfast consisting of donuts, bagels and croissants, along with some fruit, sliced cheese and deli meat. She arranged the food on a large tray.

"You're gonna spoil me and I'll never want to leave." Tony stepped into the kitchen, grabbed a grape and popped it in his mouth.

"That's the plan," Carlita said as she picked up the tray and handed it to her son. "Let's dine al fresco, out on the deck." She poured two cups of coffee and followed him outside.

Tony set the tray on the small bistro table. "When I first saw this deck, I wondered why you put it here, facing the alley, but I like it. You can see a lot from here."

Carlita handed him a cup of coffee. "Yes, you can. The alley has a life of its own. If you lean over far enough you can see out onto the street." She settled into a chair and picked up a piece of sliced turkey to share with Rambo, who promptly gobbled his treat and begged for more.

Grayvie, Carlita's cat, joined them on the deck and she gave him a slice of meat.

Tony studied his mother over the rim of his cup. "You spoil those animals."

"I know. I can't help it." Carlita changed the subject. "Today we'll work on ordering the pawnshop inventory and shelving." The two of them discussed items to stock. Carlita had already picked out the shelving. It would take a few days to arrive and then they would need to assemble it.

They discussed advertising, sidewalk signs and creating a website, which Mercedes had offered to help set up since she was much more internet savvy than her mother was.

Tony and Carlita also discussed putting together ads to bring in locals interested in selling items.

Tony shifted in his chair. "You got enough cash to buy inventory?"

Carlita thought of the gems stashed in the fireplace. She would need to pawn several stones to raise enough cash to buy pawnshop merchandise. She remembered her run-in with the owner of Paradise Pawn, Savannah's only other area pawnshop. "Remember how I mentioned the gems we found in the safe deposit box that belonged to your father? Well, I got a few big stones left. Maybe you could take them over to the local pawnshop to sell them off to raise some quick cash."

"I'll do it today," Tony said. "It's kind of ironic we're pawning stuff to raise money to buy pawnshop goods."

They finished their light breakfast and carried the food and dishes into the kitchen. "I'll hit the shower and then wake Mercedes so she can start working on the website and running ads while you head over to the pawnshop. By the time you get back, I'm hoping Annie will be free to help with our tunnel investigation."

Carlita also planned to contact Detective Zachary Jackson of the Savannah-Burnham Police Department. He had left his card with her the previous day and promised to call to let her know if they would return to wrap up the investigation.

She left a voice mail message on the number he'd given her and then headed to the bathroom to get ready.

As she showered, Carlita thought about the skeletal remains and wondered if they were linked to the boxes of gems in the basement or to George Delmario, the previous owner of her properties.

Carlita headed to the real estate office across the street as soon as she had finished getting ready. Annie was in the office with a client so Carlita waited outside until the man exited the building before she opened the door and stepped inside.

Annie rubbed her hands together. "I almost called last night to see why you needed Tinker and me this morning."

"She's been driving me crazy all morning." Cindy, Annie's receptionist, rolled her eyes.

Carlita eased into the chair in front of Annie's desk and closed her eyes. "You're never going to believe what we discovered in the basement under the pawnshop." She told the women how Tony had found the trap door and the walled off section leading into the tunnel. She also told them about the fake wall, how they had removed a section and found the skeletal remains. She left out the part about the boxes of gems. For now, Tony, Mercedes and Carlita had agreed to keep it a secret.

"Cool," Annie's eyes lit. "So where do Tinker and I fit into this?"

"We explored the tunnel last night," Carlita said. "One section was a dead end. A metal gate blocked the other section. There's something beyond the metal gate." She lifted her hands and separated them. "There's a gap at the top about this big. I think there might be enough space for Tinker to pass through and check out what's behind it."

"There's only one way to find out." Annie hopped out of her chair and darted into the hallway.

Tinker, Annie's robot, emerged from the hall and rolled into the front office. The blue lights on the front of the robot honed in on Carlita as it whirled closer. "Is that your new drone on top?" She pointed to a four-pronged plastic piece sitting atop Tinker's 'head.' At the end of the prongs were plastic blades that reminded Carlita of miniature fan blades.

"Yep." Annie nodded. "I've only tested it here in the office so I'm not sure how well it will work." She clicked the button on top of the remote control to shut Tinker off.

Carlita's cell phone chimed. It was Detective Jackson. "It's the detective investigating the case." She stepped outside and onto the sidewalk.

"Hello?"

"Mrs. Garlucci?"

"Yes. This is Carlita Garlucci."

"This is Detective Jackson. Our crime scene technicians informed me they don't plan to return to your property. They believe they have everything they need."

"Thank you for letting me know," Carlita said. "Will you call to let me know the outcome of the investigation?"

The detective assured her he would. After she disconnected the line, she stepped back inside the real estate office. "The coast is clear. Let's get this show on the road."

Chapter 9

"Elvira will be joining us," Carlita told Annie as they crossed the street.

"Elvira Cobb?" Annie stopped abruptly when they reached the sidewalk. Elvira had approached Annie first about renting an apartment from Carlita, and Annie had privately mentioned to her friend Elvira might not be a good rental candidate.

Carlita trusted Annie's advice and decided to hold out, to wait for a more suitable tenant but Elvira had other plans when she cornered Carlita and Mercedes. Next thing she knew, Elvira was moving in. So far, the decision had been a disaster, at least on Carlita's end.

"The one and only. I caught her snooping around downstairs last night. There's no way out of it." Carlita sighed heavily. "She's causing brownouts in the building. I'm certain it has something to do with this wall of computer equipment inside her apartment but I can't prove it." They reached the alley and the back door. "Let's just say there hasn't been a dull moment since she moved in."

"Speak of the devil," Annie mumbled under her breath as Carlita opened the door.

Elvira was sitting on the steps. The respirator Carlita had noticed the night before was around her neck.

Carlita pointed at the mask. "You're ready to go, I see."

"I thought you were gonna sneak down there without me. I've been waiting here for a good twenty minutes," Elvira whined. "What's that?" She pointed at Tinker.

"You'll see," Annie said. Her eyes darted to Carlita, who shrugged helplessly.

"Follow me." Carlita waved Annie and Elvira into the back room. The trap door was wide open. She leaned over the edge and peered into the darkness.

Carlita narrowed her eyes and stared at her tenant. "You promised to stay out of here until we all went down together."

Elvira held up her hand. "I swear. I didn't open the door. Maybe your hottie son did."

It couldn't have been Tony. He was on his way to *Paradise Pawn* to try to hock a few of the gems for some quick cash. Carlita had watched him leave.

"Maybe it was the detective fella," Elvira said.

"Nope. I locked the doors when we left last night." Carlita shook her head. "Detective Jackson called to tell me they won't be returning."

Annie shuffled forward and stared into the darkness. "Maybe it was someone on the other side, someone who snuck into the tunnel."

Carlita shivered involuntarily. "The only place they could've come from was…"

"The other side of the gate," Elvira and Carlita said in unison.

"I'm going for my handgun." Elvira spun on her heel and disappeared up the stairs.

"I'm going to put a lock on this today," Carlita vowed.

Elvira returned moments later, brandishing her weapon.

"Watch it with that thing!" Annie ducked as Elvira pointed the barrel of the gun at her.

"It's not loaded," Elvira whispered.

"It doesn't matter," Annie whispered back.

"Let's go." Carlita descended the steps, flashlight in hand. She waited at the bottom for the women to join her.

Annie shifted Tinker to her other arm as she eyed the dank basement warily. "This place is creepy. Where did you find the bones?"

"Over here." Carlita tiptoed across the hard packed dirt floor to the tunnel entrance. She shifted the flashlight so it illuminated the hole in the wall. "There."

Annie peeked around Carlita's shoulder. "I see what you mean." She touched one of the bricks, still in place. "The fact the hollowed out space was just on the other side of the wall is suspect."

Elvira tucked her gun in the waistband of her jeans and dropped to her knees. "Didja search for clues?"

"No. The investigators told us this area was off limits until they wrapped up their investigation." It was as if Elvira hadn't heard a word Carlita said as she crawled into the opening. A burst of bright light flashed.

"What are you doing?" Carlita hissed.

Elvira stuck her head out. "Taking pictures. I'm almost done." She disappeared back inside and there was a moment of silence.

"Ouch! I hit something sharp." A spray of loose dirt hit Carlita in the leg.

"There's something in here. I've almost got it," the woman gasped through her mask. There was a small *tink* followed by a *clunk*. Elvira emerged. "Check this out."

Annie stepped closer and peered into Elvira's grimy palm. "It looks like a ruby."

Carlita's heart skipped a beat as she stared at the stone in disbelief. The skeletal remains were linked to her, to her deceased husband, Vinnie. "I-It does." She leaned in to take a closer look.

Elvira quickly shoved the stone in her pocket and crawled deeper into the opening. "I'm almost done."

"There's no way you would get me to go inside there," Annie said.

"Me either." Perhaps it wasn't so bad having Elvira tag along after all.

"That's it." Elvira popped out of the hole and stood. "Clean as a whistle. If there was anything else inside there, the investigators already found it. Let's carry on." She plucked her gun from the front of her pants and shuffled forward. "You are going to let me keep the rock I found. It's probably not real, anyway."

Carlita was almost 100% certain it was real but she didn't dare tell Elvira that. She followed behind and Annie and Tinker brought up the rear. The tunnel didn't seem nearly as scary as it had the day before.

When they reached the fork in the tunnel, the women turned right.

"How much farther is it?" Annie slowed her pace as the tunnel narrowed.

"We're here." Elvira stopped.

Carlita angled her flashlight to the top of the gate and the opening. "Do you think Tinker's drone will fit through the gap?"

"I hope so." Annie set Tinker on the floor, reached into her back pocket and pulled out the remote control. "I'll need a spotlight on the drone to navigate through the opening."

Whir. The blades on the sides of Tinker spun and the top lifted off.

Annie carefully guided the drone along the front of the gate.

Carlita held her breath as Tinker's drone squeezed through the narrow opening and let it out when the drone was safely on the other side. "Perfect!"

Elvira and Carlita held the flashlights steady as the drone buzzed along the opening.

"I don't dare let it out of my sight." Annie pulled the lever back and the drone slowly floated along the wall. When the drone reached the point where Annie could no longer keep a visual, she turned it around and eased it back through the top of the gate.

Annie nudged the knob and the drone dropped into Carlita's outstretched hand.

"Perfect!" Carlita said. "I can't wait to see what Tinker's drone was able to record."

"Record?" Annie's eyes widened. "I was so excited, I forgot to record it."

"You didn't," Elvira groaned.

Annie grinned. "Of course not. I recorded the entire thing."

The trio retraced their steps as they made their way back inside Carlita's basement.

"I'll hold Tinker." Carlita held onto Tinker while Elvira and Annie ascended the ladder. She handed Tinker to Annie and then climbed to the top.

"Do you have time to show us what you've got?" Carlita asked.

"Yep. I'll need to borrow a laptop to plug in the cable and download the file."

"You can use mine," Elvira said.

Carlita was going to tell her they could use her computer but quickly decided she wanted to take a closer look at Elvira's arsenal of computer ware. "Let's go."

Elvira unlocked the door to her apartment and stepped aside. A whiff of sweaty feet and moldy cheese blasted Carlita in the face as she entered the living room. She waved her hand across her face. "Oh my gosh! Not again."

Annie plugged her nose and began gagging. "What in the world?"

"Natto," Elvira calmly replied. "It's a Japanese dish."

"Good for the digestive system," Carlita gasped. "You oughta smell it when she microwaves it."

"Don't knock it until you've tried it." The phone hanging on the wall next to Elvira's arsenal of equipment began to ring. "I need to answer my phone. It might be one of my customers." She hurried to the phone and lifted the receiver. "EC Investigative Services. Elvira speaking."

Carlita was dying to hear the conversation on the other end but unfortunately, her tenant didn't put the phone on speaker. "Yes. I've done some preliminary research into the three names you gave me but if you want me to do a full, in-depth investigation, other than providing you with current physical addresses, it will cost an extra fifty dollars. For sixty bucks, you'll get spouse's name, children's names, even grandchildren's names, along with the last five listed addresses and possible employers. This price includes a ten percent discount if you decide now."

Elvira grew silent. "Okay. PayPal the payment and I'll get right on it, guaranteed 24-hour turnaround or your money back." She disconnected the line and replaced the phone in the cradle. "Now where were we?"

"EC Investigative Services, huh?" Carlita pointed at the wall of equipment. "So that's what you're doing. You're running a business out of your home."

Elvira lifted her chin. "I am. There's nothing in my rental agreement that says I can't."

"I thought you worked for Savannah Architectural Society," Annie said.

"I do but it doesn't pay squat so I started my own business. Spying on people is a very lucrative business plus it's fun."

Carlita had to admit her curiosity was piqued. "How do you get your clients? I mean, if you just started this business."

"I did a ton of research and found this website. It's called 'Six-er.' Six bucks for a basic one page report but the real money is in the in-depth reports." Elvira shrugged. "Once you get the customer to call, it's easy to upsell them. Curiosity kills the cat as they say. Here's a list of my services."

Elvira snatched a sheet of paper off the desk and handed it to Carlita. Annie slid next to Carlita and they studied the sheet of paper.

EC Investigative Services – At Your Service!

Basic Research - $6.00

Employee Screening - $26.96

Tenant Screening - $46.96

Missing Person / Skip Trace - $67.56

Nanny / Childcare - $160.06

Coming Soon! Worker's Comp Surveillance

*Ask about our group discount and referral program.

Carlita wrinkled her nose and handed the sheet back. "You spy on people." She narrowed her eyes. "Have you spied on me?"

Elvira took the sheet and shrugged nonchalantly. "Maybe. Why? Do you have something to hide?"

Carlita thought about her deceased husband, Vinnie, and her "made" sons, still involved in the mafia. If she only knew, the woman would have a field day! "Not at all."

Quickly deciding she would have to be careful what information she shared with her tenant, Carlita changed the subject. "Let's take a look at what Tinker's drone was able to capture on tape during his recon mission."

Annie removed the cover on the bottom of the drone, slid the memory card out and dropped it into Elvira's hand.

Elvira slipped the card in the slot on the front of her computer and reached for her mouse.

The trio studied the screen and watched as the gate came into focus. The video blurred as the drone jerked back and forth.

"Sorry. I'm still getting the hang of handling the drone," Annie apologized.

Carlita patted her arm. "You did great. I would've crashed Tinker's drone for sure."

The footage continued and the camera recorded the top of the gate and the dark tunnel.

"I don't see anything." Carlita was disappointed.

The footage shifted as Annie began bringing the drone back to home base.

"Wait! I see something." Elvira tapped the mouse to pause the footage. "There." She pointed at the screen. "Up at the top. It looks like a portable ladder."

Sure enough, at the top of the screen was the rung of a ladder. "Too bad we can't see what's above that."

"We can." Elvira tapped the screen and the camera angle slowly panned upward until a trap door, similar to the one in Carlita's basement, appeared.

"I wonder where the door leads," Carlita mused.

"I see another one. There!" Elvira leaned forward.

"I see it too," Annie said. "It's a shame we don't know where they lead to."

Elvira shifted to the side, opened a small drawer and pulled out a folded map. "You ladies are in luck." She spread the map out on the desk. "Gather 'round."

The print was small. Carlita squinted her eyes. "I need my reading glasses."

"You can borrow this." Elvira reached under a pile of papers and pulled out a magnifying glass.

"Thanks. I think," Carlita joked.

Elvira smoothed the map. "We're right here." She tapped her finger on top of the map and then began tracing a line. "I did a little preliminary research last night."

Carlita interrupted. "I'd like to say I'm surprised."

Elvira ignored her comment. "You can see where the tunnel splits so if we follow it to the right, one of the entrances likely leads to the Parrot House Restaurant."

Annie gasped. "The other one belongs to the now closed Walton Square Souvenir store."

"Also known as the old Alder-Delaney place," Carlita finished.

Carlita set the magnifying glass next to the map. Had someone unlocked the gate and snuck into her pawnshop? A cold chill ran down her spine. Maybe she and her children weren't the only ones who knew about the stash of gems.

Chapter 10

Elvira pulled the ruby from her pocket and turned it over in her hand. "This throws a whole new light on the investigation. Think about it. First, you find the bones, hidden away behind a secret wall and then I find a ruby. If this is the real deal, it's probably worth a pretty penny and I'll bet there's a lot more where this came from."

If only she knew!

She shifted her gaze to Carlita, a gleam in her eyes. "We need to excavate, really dig around in there. Why we could be rich."

"Hypothetically speaking, suppose you're right," Carlita said. "Someone may have murdered for that gem in your hand."

"It was a long time ago," Elvira argued. "For all we know, the killer is as dead as the person behind the wall."

Carlita frowned and Elvira pressed on. "Give me a couple hours to dig around in there. If I don't find anything, I'll stop."

"I dunno." Carlita was on the fence. On the one hand, she could tell Elvira "no," but until the tunnel was re-sealed, she couldn't stop her from sneaking down there. In fact, she was almost 100% certain until the tunnel was sealed her flaky tenant would do exactly that.

"I say let her do it," Annie piped up. "What could it hurt? The investigators have wrapped up their investigation. What if there are more gems?"

A light tap on the front door saved Carlita from having to answer. "I'll think about it."

"Think fast," Elvira said as she hurried to her door, peeked through the peephole and then swung it open. "Well hello you big batch of hotness."

Carlita didn't have to look to see who was standing in the hall. It was Tony.

Tony eased past the ogling Elvira. "Hi Ma. Mercedes said she saw you come over here. I finished running my errands."

"Great!" She turned to the other women. "Give me an hour to think this over before you start digging around in the basement."

Annie followed Carlita to the door. "Tinker and I need to get back to work." She extended her hand. "I'm Annie. You must be Tony. I've heard wonderful things about you."

Tony grasped Annie's hand. "Same here."

Annie released her grip and lowered her voice. "I'll talk to you later." She shot Elvira a glance and headed down the hall.

Carlita stepped into the hall and turned to face her tenant. "Promise you'll give me an hour to make a decision on letting you dig around in the basement."

Elvira lifted her three middle fingers and tucked her thumb on top of her pinky. "Scout's honor. I'll give you an hour." She glanced at her watch.

Carlita waited until they were safely inside their apartment and the door closed. "Whew!" Carlita flopped down on the sofa and ran a hand through her hair. "You're never going to believe what we found in the basement while you were gone."

Mercedes emerged from her bedroom and wiggled in next to her mother on the sofa. "I want to hear this. If it involves Elvira, it has got to be good."

Carlita explained how Annie and Elvira had joined her to search the tunnel. Before she could stop her, Elvira had crawled into the hollowed out wall to investigate.

Mercedes rubbed the sides of her arms. "Just thinking about it gives me goosebumps. The woman is cuckoo." She twirled her finger in a circular motion next to the side of her head.

"There's more," Carlita said. "The whole hollowed out section was filled with loose dirt and I'm certain Elvira stumbled upon a gem, literally. A ruby to be exact."

"You're kidding," Tony said. "The investigators missed it?"

"It would appear so." Carlita nodded. "Now she wants to dig around inside there to see if she can find more."

"Finders keepers." Mercedes chewed on her lower lip. "So that means the gems have something to do with the skeletal remains."

"And with your father," Carlita said.

"Not to mention George Delmario," Tony added.

"That's not all," Carlita said. "The trap door leading to the basement was open when we got there."

"Someone was inside our pawnshop?" Mercedes' eyes widened.

"I think someone was inside the tunnel, came up through our trap door and onto our property," Carlita said. "Beyond the gate to the right of our tunnel are two more trap doors. Elvira somehow managed to get her hands on a diagram of Savannah's tunnel system. It appears one of the tunnels leads to the Alderson-Delaney property."

"What used to be Walton Square Souvenirs," Mercedes said.

"Correct," Carlita replied. "The other leads to who knows where. We think it may go as far as the Parrot House Restaurant."

"I have an idea." Mercedes darted into her room, returning moments later with her cell phone in hand.

"What are you doing?" Tony asked.

"I'm texting Autumn Winter to see if she's free later today." Mercedes tapped the front of the screen.

"Why?" Carlita shifted on the couch.

"Because we need to get inside the vacant property across the street to see if there are any clues," Mercedes said. Her phone chirped. "She's going to come by after work at four-thirty."

"I'm not sure you should do that," her mother said.

"It's now or never," Mercedes said. "As soon as the new owners start renovating the place, we won't be able to sneak inside and check it out."

Carlita hopped off the couch and began to pace. "You're beginning to sound like Elvira." She stopped abruptly. "By the way, Elvira started her own business and she's running it out of her apartment."

"Let me guess," Mercedes said. "She opened an art studio."

"Not even close. She started EC Investigative Services," Carlita said. "In other words, she spies on people."

Mercedes clutched her chest. "You don't think she spied on us?"

"I wouldn't put anything past her. She's probably got an entire file folder of dirt, waiting for the right moment to spring it on us."

Tony leaned forward. "She could be a lifetime tenant if she dug up even half the dirt on the Garlucci family."

It was true. Carlita's deceased husband had deep ties to the mafia. Vinnie Senior had been a "shylock," another name for a financial racketeer who loaned money at extremely inflated rates.

Carlita had done a little research and discovered that shylocks structured their loans so the debtors could never afford to pay more than the minimum interest. She also knew if the debtor failed to make the regular payment on time, the interest rate escalated. She had even heard shylocks used violence to extract payment.

She wanted to believe her Vinnie hadn't been that ruthless. Carlita also suspected it was how her husband came to acquire the Delmario family's Savannah properties.

The Garlucci family had a dark past and Elvira would have a field day. "I say we appease Elvira and let her dig around in the dirt," Mercedes said.

Knock, knock.

Carlita eyed the door warily. "Speak of the devil." She crossed the room, peeked through the peephole and then opened the door.

"Well?" Elvira stood on the other side, a pistol in one hand and a garden trowel in the other.

"After giving it some thought, I've decided you can dig around in the basement but there are a couple stipulations." Carlita lifted her index finger. "First, you need to wrap up your search in two hours or less."

"Okay." Elvira nodded.

Carlita lifted a second finger. "Two, that my son, Tony, accompany you."

Elvira grinned from ear-to-ear. "My pleasure!"

"You're kiddin'," Tony mumbled. He reluctantly slid out of the chair. "You owe me one," he muttered under his breath as he passed his mother. "Let's get this over with."

The two of them stepped into the hall and Carlita closed the door behind them. She turned to her daughter. "What if she hits the jackpot and finds more gems?"

Mercedes shrugged. "There's always the possibility. I was thinking of the tunnel and the gems. If those tunnels eventually lead out to the

Savannah River, it could be smugglers were transporting gems via ship."

Carlita sucked in a breath and closed her eyes. "We may have just opened a can of worms."

Mercedes headed to her room to research gem smuggling in Savannah while Carlita wandered into the kitchen to make sandwiches. When the sandwiches were ready, she headed down to the basement to check on Elvira and Tony.

She couldn't see them but heard muffled voices. Carlita cupped her hands and hollered down. "How's it going?"

Tony appeared at the bottom of the ladder. "So far we haven't found anything."

"Good. I mean, good for us," Carlita said. "How much longer?"

"I gave her ten more minutes." Tony glanced behind him and then stepped onto the first rung of the ladder. "I gotta hand it to her. She's very thorough. She sectioned the floor off, searching one area at a time. If she doesn't find anything, no one will."

"At least now we know. Lunch is almost ready." Carlita returned upstairs after Tony promised he would be along shortly.

Mercedes was inside, setting the table. "Well?"

"Nothing so far," Carlita reported. She strode into the kitchen, opened the refrigerator door and peered inside. "How does lemonade sound?"

"Perfect," Mercedes said.

Tony arrived home a short time later, covered in a thin layer of grime. "I'm gonna go wash up."

After they were seated at the table, Carlita turned to her son. "Well?"

"Nothing. Nada. Zip." He shook his head. "It's probably a good thing. If we'd found anything else, I don't think Elvira would give up without a fight."

"You're right. She wouldn't." Carlita reached for her turkey sandwich. "I'm not sure I'm on board with Autumn and you breaking into the place across the street."

She remembered how they'd discovered a squatter living on the first floor, below the apartments right after they'd arrived to check out their property. "What if there are homeless people living in there?"

"I've got my gun and my stun gun." Mercedes took a big bite of her sandwich and chewed loudly. "You can go with us." She eyed her brother. "You too."

"I suppose I could stand guard outside while you, your brother and Autumn do a quick search of the place."

"I want to find the tunnel." Mercedes sipped her lemonade. "If it's on the other side of the gate, like the map showed, we could check it out."

"True." Carlita grudgingly admitted her daughter had a point. She turned to Tony. "We haven't had a chance to discuss how your trip to the pawnshop went."

Tony popped the last bite of sandwich in his mouth. "Good. I met Ralph Silva, the owner of Paradise Pawn. Nice guy. He was real helpful."

"Did he know who you were?" Mercedes asked. The last time she and her mother had visited Paradise Pawn, the owner, Ralph, had informed them he intended to make sure they never got their business license. "He wasn't too keen on us when we met him."

"We had a nice long chat," Tony said. "We got to talking about back home. He has a cousin, Danny, who lives in Queens. Good guys. They're in the family, too, but not as deep. I think he said Danny was a bookie. Mostly boxing and fights in Vegas."

"Great." Carlita rolled her eyes. "Just what we need."

"Nah!" Tony waved his hand. "Don't worry about Ralph. He's on the up and up...mostly. He gave me a good price for the gems, too."

Her son leaned across the table and lowered his voice. He told me somethin' interesting. Said there was rumor of a black market smuggling ring over here close to the river. Said several of the area business owners were involved and Delmario was one of them. He ended up being investigated by the feds."

"I'm not surprised," Carlita said.

"That's not all. He said there was some kind of feud, a deal gone bad and there ended up being some bad blood between the parties."

"Which could be why the tunnel was sealed off," Mercedes said. "Maybe they used the tunnel to smuggle the goods, they got into some sort of feud and the ring broke up."

Carlita remembered how George Delmario's death was still unsolved. Perhaps a corrupt government official had swept his death under the rug or hurriedly closed the case before the investigators could uncover the truth.

"All the more reason we need to do a little more snooping around." Mercedes interrupted her mother's musings.

Tony leaned back in his chair. "Maybe Ma is right and we should let sleeping dogs lie." He shrugged. "At least now we have plenty of money to get started."

"It's too late. Autumn is already planning on coming over." Mercedes quickly changed the subject. "I have the ads ready to go. Do you want to take a look at what I came up with before I start running them?"

"Sure."

Carlita pushed her chair back. "You two take care of business and I'll clean up here." Her children disappeared into Mercedes' room to work on her computer while Carlita cleared the table.

She thought about the bones, the gems and the gate. On the one hand, she didn't want to break into the property across the street but this might be their only chance to check out the trap door and figure out what was behind the tunnel gate.

What if Pirate Pete and the Parrot House Restaurant were somehow involved? The man had seemed honest and on the up-and-up but there were times Carlita wondered if she wasn't a tad on the naïve side when it came to trusting people.

She'd never had a reason not to. Carlita and Mercedes had lived a sheltered life up until the time of Vinnie's death. She'd never even learned how to drive a car.

Now that Vinnie was gone, getting a driver's license was on Carlita's to-do list. True, it was at the bottom of her to-do list, but it was there. Baby steps. One day at a time.

Looking back over the past several months, since Vinnie's unexpected death, she'd come a long way as far as becoming independent.

Soon, she would be a business owner, a woman of her own means. Carlita was proud of all she'd accomplished in a short amount of time. Deep down, she knew if Vinnie were still alive, he would be proud of her, too.

She remembered her vow to Vinnie on his deathbed, how he'd made her promise to get their children, their sons, out of the "family." So far, she'd only managed to get herself and Mercedes out.

Carlita prayed Vinnie, Jr. would come out of hiding soon so she could talk to him, make him see his life could be so much better if he turned away from a life of crime.

The fact Tony was here meant his brother had told him it wasn't such a bad place after all. Carlita had hinted around to her middle son that he should move to Savannah. She hadn't come right out and asked, hoping he would reach that conclusion on his own.

Carlita finished placing the dirty glasses in the dishwasher and shut the door. Until Vinnie came out of hiding, all she could do was pray and wait.

She glanced at the clock on the stove. It was almost time for Autumn to show up so they could get the investigation underway.

Chapter 11

Mercedes wrinkled her nose and pointed at Autumn's backpack. "You don't think crawling into an abandoned building carrying a backpack will look suspicious?"

Autumn patted the backpack. "It's a necessity. Our supplies are in here." She ticked off the list. "Flashlights, rubber gloves, zip-lock baggies for evidence, EMF meter."

Carlita held up a hand. "What in the world is an EMF meter?"

"It's an electromagnetic frequency meter. I read the Alder-Delaney place has had a ton of ghost sightings so I borrowed the EMF meter from my buddy at work. He said this baby can detect high levels of EMF and swears when you get a reading, you're close to a ghost."

Autumn grinned. "Hey! Did you catch that? Close to a ghost. Haha. I also brought a hand shovel in case we need to dig. Speaking of dig, did your psycho tenant find anything else?"

"Nope." Mercedes shook her head.

Tony had been out on the patio with Rambo. He made his way inside and over to his sister and her friend.

"Oh! I almost forgot. Autumn, this is my older brother, Tony."

Autumn grinned, a twinkle in her blue eyes. "How many good looking brothers do you have?"

"Good looking is debatable but I have three altogether. Paulie, the youngest brother but still older than me, is married. He lives in Clifton Falls with his wife, Gina, and my two nieces and nephew."

Autumn shook his hand. "Speaking of good looking brothers how is Vinnie? I haven't heard you mention him lately."

Mercedes and her mother exchanged a quick glance. "He's doing all right, as far as we know."

Tony snorted. "Right."

Carlita elbowed him and quickly changed the subject. "It sounds as if you've come prepared, Autumn. We better get this mission under way before I change my mind."

"Righto." Mercedes snapped her fingers. "I'll be right back." She hurried to her room and returned moments later wearing a different shirt with a noticeable bulge in the front.

Her mother pointed at the bulge. "Tell me that's not your gun."

"It's not my gun," Mercedes said.

Carlita leaned forward and lifted the edge of her daughter's blouse. "Yes it is."

"I know, but you told me to tell you it wasn't," Mercedes said with a straight face. "I told you what you wanted to hear. We need protection. Who knows what we're going to run into."

"I've got mine, too." Tony patted his jacket pocket.

"Me three," Autumn admitted.

"Good heavens. How many guns do we need?" Carlita asked.

"Three." Mercedes, Tony and Autumn said in unison.

Carlita rolled her eyes heavenward. "Lord, please help us make it through this without anyone getting shot."

"Or slimed by a ghost," Autumn joked.

***

Carlita shaded her eyes and stared at the back of the building. The days were growing shorter now that fall was right around the corner and soon it would be dark. Shadows filled the alley as the tall buildings blocked what was left of the daylight.

Her eyes traveled up and she stared at the building's dark windows. A feeling someone was staring at them washed over Carlita. "I dunno about this."

"It's now or never." Mercedes tugged on her mother's arm and led her to the stoop in the back. "Besides, all you gotta do is stand guard and let us know if anyone shows up."

Carlita gazed from her daughter, to her son, to Autumn. "For the record, I'm against this."

"We'll be fine Mrs. G." Autumn dropped her backpack, unzipped the top, reached inside and pulled out a slim jim. "I've been practicing my window unlocking technique." She hurried over to the window, slipped the tool in the gap between the frames and tapped it to the side.

Carlita's armpits grew damp as she gazed down the alley, certain someone would catch them in the act at any moment.

"It's. Not. Working." Autumn jerked the tool up and the window frame groaned in protest as it made a small snapping sound.

"You're gonna bust the window," Tony said as he held out his hand. "Let me try."

Autumn dropped the tool in his hand and stepped aside.

Tony deftly slid the slim jim into the frame and with one quick motion popped the window lock. He handed the tool back to Autumn. "Sometimes you gotta leave it to the pros."

Carlita glared at her son and shook her head.

"I'm kidding." Tony lifted the window and shifted to the side. "Ladies first."

Mercedes stepped to the window, placed both hands on the frame and pulled herself up and over. For a moment, her feet dangled in the air before she disappeared from sight. "Ugh. I'm in."

"I do believe you girls are getting way too good at breaking into buildings," Carlita groaned as she watched Autumn mimic Mercedes' move and disappeared inside.

Tony's approach was slightly different. He grabbed a rusty paint can sitting near the edge of the building, set it under the center of the sill, stepped on top and climbed inside before turning back. "If we don't return in half an hour, call the cops."

Carlita's mouth fell open. "You're kidding! You want me to call the police and tell them you broke into this place and you never came back out?"

"Of course I'm kiddin'." Tony shook his head and patted his jacket pocket where he'd placed his gun. "Don't worry. We'll be back."

Carlita watched her son disappear into the shadows. She turned to face the alley. The feeling she was being watched came rushing back. Her eyes slid to the building directly across the narrow strip of real estate.

A small puff of steam emerged from the vent. The smell of household bleach wafted in the air. She squinted her eyes and studied the structure.

The building appeared to be empty, too, except for the steam, a dead giveaway that someone was inside the building. *I need to stop getting involved with dead bodies.*

Kachink. Carlita spun back around and gazed through the open window. The faint sound had come from inside the building. "Tony?" she hissed under her breath.

There was no answer but the sound of a faint creak coming from the upper floor.

The thump of Carlita's heart beating in her chest drowned out the creaks and she prayed they would finish quickly. The sensation of being watched intensified and the hair on the back of her neck stood up.

She started to shift to the side when she caught a glimpse of an ominous figure out of the corner of her eye, right before a heavy hand clutched her right shoulder.

Chapter 12

"I say we start down here. It's the emptiest and we can move fast," Mercedes said.

"I agree," Autumn said.

The trio parted ways with Mercedes heading to the front of the building; the section that once housed Walton Square Souvenirs. The only thing she found was a thick layer of dust and piles of dust bunnies crowding the corners.

Mercedes swiped her hand across an empty glass shelf and a plume of dust filled the air.

A...choo! She rubbed the back of her hand across her nose and tiptoed forward. The *Walton Square Souvenirs* logo was still etched on the front window.

As she passed by the front door, she stopped to check to make sure the door was locked.

Although the door was locked, the deadbolt wasn't latched. "That's odd," she mumbled.

The rest of the room was empty so she made her way down the small hall to the back room where she found Autumn examining a row of metal shelves.

"Anything of interest?"

Autumn wrinkled her nose. "No. There's nothing here but a bunch of junk. This place needs a bulldozer." She picked up a piece of rusty metal. It reminded Mercedes of a small saw blade. "Check this out. This looks like blood."

Mercedes lifted the edge of her blouse and took the metal piece from Autumn. "Nah. I think it's rust. Why would a shop owner who sells trinkets and souvenirs need something like this?"

"I dunno." Autumn pointed at one of the shelves. "There's a whole stack of them."

Mercedes shuffled to the edge of the metal shelf and dropped the metal piece on top before pulling her cell phone from her back pocket and turning it on.

"What are you doing?"

"Taking a picture in case your very vivid imagination is correct and this is blood."

"Yeah and someone used these blades as instruments of torture," Autumn shuddered.

"That's creepy," Mercedes said.

"You find anything yet?" A deep voice echoed from the doorway causing Mercedes to jump. "You scared me half to death!"

"This place is givin' me the heebie-jeebies, too," Tony said. "I didn't find nothin'. Let's head upstairs before Ma calls the cops."

The trio retraced their steps to the end of the hall and the stairs leading to the upper level. Tony led the way, Autumn followed behind and

Mercedes brought up the rear. The wooden steps creaked loudly from their weight as they climbed.

Mercedes' stomach churned as the smell of stagnant air mixed with a metallic odor filled the space. "This space smells funky."

"I agree." Autumn pinched her nose. "Let's hurry and get this over with."

The upper level was one large, cavernous space. A silhouette of stud walls lined one side and a grimy porcelain toilet sat in the corner. In the opposite corner was a small stack of boxes.

"I wonder what's inside the boxes." Autumn removed her backpack, set it on the floor, reached inside and pulled out a flashlight. She flipped it on and bright light illuminated the dim interior.

"You first." Autumn handed the flashlight to Tony.

Tony strode across the open space. He held the flashlight in one hand while he tugged on the corner of the box with the other.

Inside the box was a black grinding wheel. There was also a stack of blades, similar to the one the girls had found downstairs.

Once again, Mercedes took her phone from her pocket and snapped several pictures.

"Why don't we take the goods with us?" Tony asked as he watched his sister.

"One, because that's stealing and two, because the new...old owners may have already inspected the building's contents and might notice something's missing."

"This old box of junk?" Tony kicked the box with the tip of his shoe.

"We need to take a peek inside the basement before we leave," Autumn said.

The trio descended the steps and rounded the corner with Tony leading the way. "The trapdoor is under the stairwell." He knelt down and flashed the light into the stairwell. "Check it out. It looks like someone has already been down here not too long ago."

Mercedes leaned in. He was right. The trap door was dust free, unlike the rest of the floor. "Maybe someone is living down there." Visions of a homeless person occupying the dark, dank basement filled her head.

"They would be crazy," Autumn said.

Tony grasped the trap door latch, a crude notch in the wood and lifted it up. He leaned the top against the wall and adjusted the flashlight. "This has one of those retractable ladders." He set the flashlight on the floor and unlatched the ladder. It clattered loudly before hitting the floor below.

"You're going to wake the dead," Mercedes hissed.

Tony ignored the comment as he grabbed his flashlight and took a step down. "You comin' or not?"

Mercedes glanced at her brother and sucked in a deep breath. "I guess so."

Autumn followed Tony. She looked up at her friend, still hovering uncertainly near the opening. "It's okay. I'll protect you." She waved at her friend.

"I'm getting a bad feeling about this." Mercedes slowly descended the ladder and then hurried to Autumn and Tony's side.

Tony shined the flashlight around the cramped space. "Our main goal is to confirm this tunnel ends at the gate we found. It should be this way."

The trio crept across the basement and made their way into the tunnel. It was a short distance before the tunnel forked. They continued to the right in what they hoped was the direction of the metal gate.

Tony stopped abruptly. "This is it." He beamed the light toward the now familiar black gate. "Let's backtrack and see what we can find in the other direction." They passed the basement moments later.

Mercedes' steps began to drag. Her gut told her they were walking into a trap. She pulled her gun from the waistband of her pants and clutched it in a tight grip.

Tony stopped abruptly. "Whatcha doin' waving that thing around?"

"I'm not waving it." Mercedes waved the gun. "Sorry. This place is freaking me out. I feel like we're walking into some sort of trap."

Autumn clutched Tony's arm. "Maybe she's right. We could end up buried in the wall, just like the person you found."

"Not without a fight," Tony growled. "If you two are too chicken, stay here. I'm gonna keep goin'."

"I can't let you die alone," Mercedes answered bravely as she picked up the pace to catch up with her brother.

The tunnel opened up into what appeared to be another basement. Two small square windows faced each other. Dim shafts of light filtered through a thick layer of grime covering the windows. The basement was empty except for a set of narrow steps that ran up the side of one wall.

Tony crept up the steps and pushed on the trap door. It wouldn't budge.

"These steps remind me of the ones in the Parrot House Restaurant's basement." He made his way back down the steps. "It's the end of the road ladies. The trap door is locked." Tony shined his flashlight along the side of the crumbling wall.

"At least we're still alive," Mercedes said as she shifted her flashlight. She pointed to a fresh set of muddy tracks leading up the steps. "Tony, do you have mud on your shoes?"

He lifted his shoe to examine the bottom. "Nope. Those tracks aren't mine."

Mercedes grabbed her cell phone and snapped a picture of the muddy prints.

"We hit a dead end, literally," Autumn said. "We might as well head back. I'm sure your mother is worried sick something happened to us."

They turned to go when something caught Mercedes' eye. "Wait!" she whispered as she pointed at the far corner of the basement. "Check it out."

Tony spun around and followed his sister's gaze.

"There's a narrow tunnel over there."

Whirp...whirp.

Mercedes jumped. "What was that?"

"It's my EMF meter." Autumn slipped her backpack off, unzipped the front and reached inside. "It's detecting some sort of electromagnetic field." She held the machine at arm's length and then slowly spun in a circle. "It's coming from this direction." She shuffled forward. The *whirping* noise grew louder and the *whirps* closer together. "I think it's right here."

"Eek!" Autumn let out a small squeak and loosened her grip on the meter. "A cold blast of air blew past me."

"I'm out of here." Mercedes made a mad dash into the tunnel and to the other basement. She scrambled up the ladder, raced across the back of the vacant building and catapulted herself through the open window where she came face-to-face with her mother and a person she never expected to see.

Chapter 13

"What are you doing here?" Mercedes gasped as she staggered to regain her balance.

Elvira Cobb crossed her arms and rolled back on her heels. "What am *I* doing here? What are you doing? Breaking into someone else's property?"

Autumn scrambled through the open window and jumped to her feet, still holding the EMF meter. "Whoa."

Tony was the last to emerge via the window and he calmly nodded at Elvira. "Hello Elvira."

"Hello Toneee." Elvira patted her hair and batted her eyes. "I had no idea you were involved in this criminal activity, too. Well? Did you find anything? Were you able to figure out where the tunnel ended?"

The trio explained their hunch had been correct. Mercedes told her mother and Elvira the metal gate blocked access to their property across the street and there was another trap door located at the end of the tunnel, not to mention a second, smaller passageway they weren't able to explore because Autumn's EMF meter went off.

"Do you have any idea who the other trap door belongs to?" Elvira asked.

"Tony said he's almost certain it connects to the Parrot House," Mercedes said. "We couldn't verify it though because the trap door was locked."

"Then I got a major reading on my EMF." Autumn held up the meter. "There was definitely some sort of presence at the end of the tunnel."

"I bet it was a ghost who can float right through those iron bars and he visits our basement all the time," Tony teased.

Mercedes slugged her brother in the arm. "That is not funny!"

Carlita lifted her hand. "Stop. Both of you. Just the thought creeps me out." She turned to Elvira. "You never did tell me how you figured out we were over here."

Elvira tapped the side of her forehead with her index finger. "You've got to get up pretty early in the morning to pull one over on Elvira Cobb. The Segway and your car were still at the apartment so I figured you hadn't gone too far." She lowered her hand. "The cop, what's his name, stopped by to update you on the remains they found in your basement."

"I'll give Detective Jackson a call when I get home," Carlita said.

"No need. He gave me a written report of the findings." Elvira pulled a folded sheet of paper from her pocket and waved it in the air. "Very interesting indeed."

Mercedes snatched the paper out of Elvira's hand. "He gave it to you? Why would the detective give the report to you?"

"Because Carlita is my sister," Elvira calmly explained. "We're family and co-owners."

"You lied to the detective?" Carlita gasped.

Elvira shrugged. "You have a problem with that? You committed a crime by breaking and entering someone else's property."

Carlita placed her head in her hands. "I give up. What does it say?"

"It's a bunch of mumbo jumbo." Mercedes handed the sheet to her mother.

Elvira cleared her throat. "Ahem. I dabbled in forensic osteology back in the day."

"I'm not surprised," Carlita said.

Elvira sniffed. "From what I could glean, based on the composition of the body, the environment in which it decomposed and several other factors, the results were inconclusive, other than the fact the deceased was female and you couldn't have killed her due to the age of the remains."

"In other words, they don't know," Autumn said.

"Bingo." Elvira nodded. She turned to Tony. "So you found another trap door and you think it leads to the Parrot House Restaurant? It makes sense." She rubbed her hands together. "Too bad we can't take a lookee see at the place."

"We've already been there," Carlita argued. "Pirate Pete was kind enough to show us the basement. He didn't appear to be hiding anything."

"Those are the ones you gotta watch out for," Elvira said as she nodded toward the building Tony, Mercedes and Autumn had exited. "What's the 411 on this place? You find anything useful?"

Mercedes remembered the saw blades with rust/blood and the polishing tools but quickly decided to keep quiet about the tools. "Nothing stood out. The place is clean."

"Vicki Munroe, the Savannah Architectural Society veep told me one of the original family members purchased the property from Ruby McKinley after you ran her off."

"I did not run that woman off," Carlita argued. "She was nothing but a troublemaker."

"Anyhoo, rumor round town is they plan to fix it up and turn it into a haunted bed and breakfast. Sweet Magnolia Bed & Breakfast. You couldn't pay me to stay there, knowing how Alder's first wives died mysteriously and one of them vanished." Elvira pointed at Autumn's EMF meter. "Surprised that baby didn't go off the charts inside the place."

"If it did, I didn't hear it." Autumn stared at the small handheld device. "I guess I didn't think to check."

"The window of opportunity is still unlocked. We could give it a go." Elvira took a step toward the window.

Carlita clamped her hand around Elvira's wrist. "Oh no. We should let sleeping dogs, or in this case, ghosts, rest."

"Party pooper," Elvira said. "Guess it doesn't really matter. Ghosts don't kill people. People kill people. I'm putting my money on either the Alder-Delaney gang or someone from the Parrot House Restaurant."

"Or the previous owners of my property," Carlita said quietly. She mulled over the new information as they slowly made their way home. Were the Alder-Delaney descendants returning to the scene of a family crime? Perhaps it was Pirate Pete. It was possible he was the gatekeeper of the tunnels since his was one of the last in line to reach the river.

She thought about the gems. Was Pirate Pete and the others in on the gem smuggling?

There was also the mystery of the unidentified remains. The fact James Alder's third wife had mysteriously disappeared caused Carlita to wonder if the bones were hers.

The fleeting thought something even more sinister, something that involved her beloved Vinnie, the gems and the Delmario family flooded her mind. She quickly pushed the thoughts aside.

There was a connection somewhere between the gems, the tunnels and the poor woman. Now all they had to do was figure out how the three were linked.

Chapter 14

Carlita wasn't in the mood to cook a large dinner and convinced her children they should order Chinese and have it delivered.

While they waited for their delivery, Mercedes wandered into her room. Tony moved his laptop to the dining room table to do a little more research on the pawnshop and check on the status of the ordered equipment.

Carlita settled into the computer nook Mercedes and she had set up right after her daughter surprised her with a new laptop. She was finding her way around the internet and having fun doing it.

Every once in a while, she would get hung up and Mercedes would come to her rescue, but it was getting easier and she'd even found a website to borrow e-books to read in her free time.

According to the report Detective Jackson had given Elvira, the investigation was still open but from what she could glean, it was no longer a high priority.

One the one hand, Carlita was all for not stirring the pot but on the other, deep down, she had to know…had her husband somehow been involved in the woman's death? Had he been involved in George Delmario's demise?

Maybe she didn't want to know. It would tarnish her memory of her beloved. She also wondered if the new owners, the Alder descendants, had heard about the discovery of the bones.

Carlita fired up her computer and clicked on the Savannah Evening News. The story of the skeletal remains found in their basement was no longer a headliner. A brief blurb stated the female appeared to be in her mid-thirties at the time of her death and the reason for her death inconclusive.

Carlita shifted in her chair. "We're going to seal up that tunnel." It wasn't a question, but merely a reminder to her son.

"Sure Ma. I can do it tomorrow if you want."

"The sooner the better." Carlita turned her attention back to the article and then clicked out of the screen. She typed in 'James Alder' death and found a small story written about Alder. He arrived in Savannah from England, Dover to be exact. Carlita had never heard of the place.

It explained how he'd been a sea merchant by trade and had been married twice before moving to the United States. Both wives died under mysterious circumstances. He met his third wife, Mary Beth Delaney, after moving to Savannah.

James Alder's death had been by natural causes. He died at the ripe old age of 91.

Carlita wondered how Alder's first wives had died and what had happened to his third wife, Mary Beth.

Tony interrupted his mother's musings. "Hey! Looks like all our goods are in transit. We should be able to start working on setting up shop day after tomorrow."

"That's wonderful news." Carlita smiled as she noted the look of excitement on her son's face. He was finally coming around. "So you're going to stay and help me run Savannah Swag?"

Tony slowly shook his head. "I dunno Ma. I promise I'll stay long enough to get you up and running."

Buriing. The outer doorbell chimed. "That must be our dinner." Carlita hopped out of the chair but Tony beat her to the door. "I'll take care of it." He disappeared into the hall while Carlita headed to the kitchen to grab some plates, drinks and silverware.

"Dinner is ready," Carlita hollered toward the hall as she made her way to the dining room table. She carefully set Tony's laptop off to one side to make room for the food and caught a glimpse of the screen. It displayed a listing of local Savannah restaurants.

Tony returned with the bags of food and closed the door behind him.

Carlita pulled out a chair. "Are you taking your Ma somewhere special for dinner?" She pointed to the open laptop screen.

The tips of Tony's ears reddened. "Nah. I was...uh...talking to Shelby next door. I ran into her in the hall this morning. She seems like such a nice lady, kinda down on her luck without much money. I figured I would invite her to dinner."

Mercedes bounced into the room. "Oh! A date. We can watch Violet if you want. Right Mom?"

Carlita pulled the top container of food from the bag. "Of course. When do you plan to take her?"

"Maybe tomorrow night," he said. "I thought I'd stop by later tonight to ask her."

"Sounds like a wonderful thing to do," Carlita said. She reached out and patted his hand. "Remember, it appears she's married."

"Yeah." Tony reached for an egg roll. "It's not like a date or nothin'. I'm taking her as a friend."

"Of course." Carlita eased a large spoonful of vegetable lo mein onto her plate. "Let us know if our services are needed." She left it at that and they changed the subject to discuss Savannah Swag.

Mercedes took a big swig of Diet Coke. "Autumn volunteered to help. She said Steve offered to help, too."

"You haven't met Steve," Carlita told her son. "Steve is Autumn's older brother. I think he has a crush on Mercedes."

Mercedes' face turned two shades of red. "He does not," she mumbled.

"Hmm." Her mother answered noncommittally. "What are you working on in the bedroom?"

"I'm finishing up a small project," Mercedes said. "After dinner, I'm going to research the tunnels myself, see if I can figure out where the smaller tunnel we didn't get a chance to explore, leads to."

Carlita added a scoop of chicken fried rice to her plate and shared a small piece with Grayvie, who was doing circle eights around her legs in an attempt to get her attention.

Rambo waited for Carlita to share her food with Grayvie before trying a different approach. He stared at Carlita. Not blinking.

"I'd give you a small piece of chicken but you'd inhale it in one second. Let me get you a treat." Carlita slid out of the chair, grabbed a handful of bite size doggie treats and fed them to Rambo, who rewarded her by licking her hand.

After they finished eating, Carlita reached for her empty plate. "I can clean up if you want to run next door to chat with Shelby."

"Thanks Ma." Tony kissed his mother's cheek and then made his way out of the apartment.

"I've never seen him this interested in a woman." Mercedes carried the leftovers to the kitchen and placed them inside the refrigerator. "I'd like to do a little more research and then we can take Rambo for a walk."

Rambo's ears perked up and he thumped his tail on the kitchen floor.

"Sounds good." Carlita rinsed the drink glasses and set them inside the dishwasher. She had just finished wiping the table and kitchen counters when Mercedes ran into the room.

"You're never going to guess what I found on the internet."

Chapter 15

Carlita draped the wet dishrag on the sink divider and turned to her daughter. "What did you find?"

"I found an online video showing the locations where you can access Savannah's underground tunnels from the street."

"No way," Carlita said.

"Yep." Mercedes nodded. "Check this out."

Carlita followed her daughter into her bedroom and to desk in the corner.

Mercedes slid into the chair, reached for the mouse and clicked on the screen.

Carlita leaned in. She watched as two women and two men stood on a sidewalk. One of the men knelt down and removed a manhole cover. The video was a little grainy but sure enough, the four people disappeared inside the manhole and into an underground tunnel. "I can't hear anything."

"Whoops! Sorry!" Mercedes tapped the mouse to turn the volume up.

One of the women, a blonde, faced the camera. She was holding a microphone. "This is Valerie Zarkowski reporting from Channel 10 News. Many Savannah residents have no idea there are several manholes, located throughout the Historic Savannah district, that lead to a maze of underground tunnels."

She went on to explain city workers used the access points to maintain the sewer systems. Not only were the tunnels used by city workers, but also by vagrants and the city's homeless as makeshift shelters.

The camera panned to show a filthy mattress, a pair of dirty sneakers and a portable cooktop stove.

According to the news reporter, city officials and charitable organizations made regular attempts to reach the people who lived underground to persuade them to move to area shelters but most resisted and even if they were talked into leaving, they would eventually return.

"Pirate Pete was right," Carlita shook her head. "Those poor people. We need to help."

"I agree," Mercedes said. "At the end of the video is a list of places we can contact to help. I wouldn't mind volunteering."

The video ended a short time later and Carlita's stomach churned as the images on the screen played in her head. She wondered what caused a person to reach a point in their life where they chose to live on the streets, or in this case, under the streets.

Tony returned to the apartment a short time later, grinning like the cat that swallowed the canary.

"I take it you have a date tomorrow night," Mercedes teased.

"Shh." Tony held a finger to his lips. "I do not have a date. I am having dinner with a new friend. You're making a mountain out of a molehill."

"Shelby is okay with Violet visiting with us while you're on your da…er, dining together?" Carlita asked.

"Yeah. Violet got so excited she went to her room to pack her backpack she plans to bring with her." Tony shook his head. "Poor Rambo and Grayvie. That little girl has more energy in her pinky than I have in my whole body."

Carlita smiled. She was looking forward to spending time with Violet and getting to know both her and her mother. "We'll have a ball. Maybe we can bake some cookies."

She switched the subject. "What about the husband?" The last thing Carlita wanted was for her son to be caught in the middle of a marital dispute.

Tony stepped away from the front door and lowered his voice. "I was gonna ask Shelby but she beat me to the punch. Her divorce finalized the day she moved out of the women's shelter and into the apartment."

Carlita was visibly relieved. Not only did she not want her son to end up caught in the middle of a domestic dispute, she didn't want to see him end up with a broken heart, although in the past, Tony had been the heartbreaker, not the heartbroken. In fact, he'd left a trail of broken hearts back in Queens. "You're not going to lead Shelby on and then dump her," she said bluntly.

"Ma!" Tony growled. "It will be two new friends having dinner together. Nothing less. Nothing more."

"Just checking." Carlita reached for Rambo's leash. "Mercedes and I are taking Rambo for a walk. Would you like to join us?"

"I was gonna hang out at home and watch the pawnshop television show I recorded to see if I could pick up a few pointers unless you want me to go with you," Tony said.

"Nah. We won't be long," Carlita said.

The women slipped out of the apartment and Carlita gave Elvira's door a quick glance. She briefly wondered if the woman was somehow spying on them, watching their every move.

She tugged on her daughter's arm, hoping to avoid another encounter with Elvira. At the bottom of the stairs, they passed by Mercedes' Segway. "Would you like to take your Segway?"

"Nah. I still wish you'd give it a go or at the very least sign up for driver's training," Mercedes said. "Someday you're going to get tired of walking everywhere."

"I will. I promise before Christmas, I'll get my driver's license. It'll be one of my Christmas presents to you so you don't have to worry about me." Carlita breathed a sigh of relief when they reached the alley and Elvira was nowhere in sight.

"I only worry because if something happened to me, you'd be stuck," Mercedes said. "Plus, you might actually discover you like driving."

Carlita seriously doubted that would happen. Although the thought terrified her, she'd been giving herself little pep talks, telling herself she could do it, she would do it, if not for her own sake, for Mercedes' sake.

If she could move hundreds of miles away from the only home she'd ever known and start a business she knew nothing about, she could certainly learn how to drive a car. "You're right Mercedes. As soon as I get Savannah Swag up and running, I'm going to let you start giving me driving lessons.

"Great!" Mercedes said. "Now let's scope out those riverfront properties before it gets dark."

Chapter 16

"Check that out."

"What?"

"The Cobblestone Bed & Breakfast." Mercedes pointed to the building adjacent to the Parrot House Restaurant. "I would love to take a peek inside. This place is close to the river, even closer than the Parrot House."

Carlita glanced at the Parrot House Restaurant. Perhaps several of the Walton Square business owners had once been involved in a gem smuggling ring. They were in the perfect location…the Parrot House Restaurant, the Cobblestone Bed & Breakfast, her property, not to mention the old Alder-Delaney place.

All four places connected via the tunnel. Carlita had a feeling they were only scratching the surface, literally, and that there was more, much more than met the eye when it came to some of the past and present business owners of Walton Square.

Despite the growing mystery, Carlita had enough to worry about, between trying to get the pawnshop up and running, deciding what to do about her last vacant apartment, not to mention making sure her past, her husband's past, stayed buried.

"I think we should let this whole gem mystery go," Carlita told her daughter after they crossed to the other side of the street. "We have enough troubles. For all we know, we could be stirring up a hornet's nest."

"You think so? I mean, I think we're onto something." Mercedes loved the mystery, the intrigue. In fact, she loved it so much; she was taking notes for her next novel. She had put the finishing touches on her debut novel, *Murder, Mayhem and the Mafia, a Mob Daughter's*

Confessions. This new mystery gave her some fresh material she planned to use for a sequel book.

"The least we can do is go over everything we have so far," Mercedes argued. "We've invested a lot of time and I'd like to at least try to put the pieces of the puzzle together. We haven't even had a chance to look at the pictures I've taken."

"Okay." Carlita caved. Her daughter was right, to a point. What harm would it do to look at all of the information they'd gathered? "We can do it in the morning. It's been a long day and my mind is mush."

It was a short walk to their back alley. Carlita reached in her pocket for her set of keys when she noticed a dim light coming from the back window of the pawnshop. "Tony must've forgotten to turn the lights off."

She unlocked the back door, and Rambo and Mercedes followed her into the back room. She reached around the corner to flip the lights off when something caught her eye. The trap door was wide open.

Carlita tiptoed to the edge of the opening. "Tony? Are you down there?"

The sound of rustling echoed through the opening. It was followed by two short *thump, thumps.*

Clang. The faint sound of metal clanging preceded a faint click.

Carlita's heart began to pound fiercely in her chest. "Who's down there?"

Silence.

Rambo's nails clicked on the wooden floor as he shifted closer to the opening and began to growl.

Woof!

Carlita turned to her daughter. "Run upstairs and get your brother."

"I'll do one better. I'll call him." Mercedes switched her cell phone on, scrolled the screen, pressed the call button and hit the speaker.

"Hello?" Tony's voice echoed through the line.

"Where are you?"

"I'm in the apartment. Where are you?"

"Mom and I are down in the shop. The trap door is open and we hear noises coming from the basement. It sounds like someone is down there."

"I'm on my way." The line went dead.

Heavy footsteps tore down the stairs and Tony burst into the room carrying a baseball bat. "I locked this place up tighter than a drum not more than an hour ago. You sure you heard something?"

"Yes and not only that, the light was on and the door was wide open."

Mercedes pointed at the bat. "You gave up on the gun?"

"Nah! It was the first thing I saw so I grabbed it on my way out." Tony shifted the bat to his other hand and started down the ladder. "Stay here."

Carlita nodded fearfully and began to pray for her son's safety. He disappeared from sight and she held her breath as she waited for him to return.

Moments later, he reappeared and stood at the bottom of the ladder. "Whoever was down here is gone now. You musta scared them off."

Tony lifted his hand. "They left in such a hurry they dropped this."

Carlita squinted her eyes and gazed at her son's outstretched hand. "What is it?"

"It's a flashlight." Tony shoved the flashlight in his front pocket and gripped the bat as he climbed the ladder. "I heard shuffling coming from beyond the metal gate but when I hollered, no one answered."

"So someone was definitely in our basement." A wave of fear washed over Carlita. "We need to seal the tunnel pronto."

"Tomorrow," Tony nodded. "Now that we have proof someone is creeping around here, we need to secure the property." He pointed to the small slide lock on the outside of the trap door. "If someone wants in here bad enough, it would be easy for them to bust this lock."

"We could nail it shut," Mercedes suggested.

"If we do that, we'll have to open it back up again tomorrow. We need something heavy to place on top of the door." Tony's eyes scanned the empty room.

"I have an old steamer trunk in the living room. We could drag it down here."

"It'll have to do." Tony dropped the trap door and slid the lock into place.

The trio headed up the stairs. With Tony on the back end and Carlita and Mercedes on the front end, they slid the trunk down the steps and half-carried, half-dragged it to the trap door.

"This thing is heavy," Mercedes gasped. "If they can break the bolt and knock this trunk off the top then they're super human."

"True." Carlita straightened her back. "We've done all we can do for tonight."

Tony checked the doors and windows before the three of them headed up the stairs and into their apartment.

Carlita eased into the recliner, leaned her head back and closed her eyes. "I'm whupped." She lifted her head and studied her son, who had grabbed the remote and settled onto the couch. "Do you think we're cursed?"

"Whatdya mean cursed?" Tony turned to his mother.

"I mean your father's unexpected death not to mention someone breaking into our house in Queens. Within minutes of arriving here, we find a dead woman next door and now this. Maybe we're cursed. I'm cursed."

"No way Ma. Pops was, well, we both know he was no saint. I'm not sayin' he was asking for trouble, although there was a rumor going 'round maybe someone whacked him." Tony shrugged. "The others are just coincidental. You told me the broad you found in the other property was dead before you ever got here. Same thing with the bones we found in the basement."

Tony switched the television on and lowered the volume. "Maybe you're the cleanup crew. You know. Someone else does the deed and you follow behind cleaning up after them."

"The last thing I want is to be a cleanup crew." Carlita leaned forward in her chair. "They say everything happens in threes. George Delmario's body was found out back by the dumpster - unsolved murder. Norma Jean Cleaver - solved murder."

"Thanks to you," Tony interjected.

"Now we have this poor woman whose body has been hidden behind the basement wall for decades." Carlita stood. "My head is spinning. I think I'll turn in for the night. I have a feeling tomorrow is going to be a long day."

If only she knew how long it would be.

***

Carlita tossed and turned all night. Each time she woke, she glanced at the clock and the hours crawled by. When she slept, she dreamt of Vinnie. In one of her dreams, Vinnie was alive. He was leading her through the tunnel. The dream seemed so real. She begged him not to go into the tunnel, telling him it was dangerous, but he wouldn't listen.

When they reached the gate, they discovered it was unlocked. She grabbed her husband's arm and pleaded with him not to go through the gate but he ignored her and stepped to the other side.

A dark, sinister figure appeared out of nowhere and loomed over the top of Vinnie.

"Vinnie! Watch out!" Carlita screamed.

The image vanished into thin air and Vinnie lay sprawled out on the dirt floor.

She darted through the open gate to her husband's side where she fell to her knees and leaned over him. "Vinnie!"

Vinnie's vacant eyes were wide open. The expression on his face was one of sheer terror.

Carlita sat upright in bed, her eyes darting around her dark bedroom. She quickly flipped her small bedside lamp on and clutched her blankets to her chest. It was 5:45 in the morning.

She willed herself to relax, telling herself it was only a bad dream. When her breathing returned to normal, she shut the light off and attempted to go back to sleep but Vinnie's eyes were there, staring back at her.

Carlita finally gave up. She crawled out of bed, slipped her bathrobe on and crept into the hall.

Tony was already awake. She could see his silhouette on the patio. He was smoking a cigarette.

Carlita shuffled to the patio door and eased it open. The acrid smell of cigarette smoke curled in the air. "I thought you were trying to quit smoking."

"I am." Tony shifted to the side. "Some days are better than others." He dropped the cigarette in a Dixie cup half-full of water and blew the plume of smoke toward the alley.

Carlita reached down and patted Rambo, who was sprawled out on the deck. "I hope you don't take up smoking," she joked and then turned her attention to her son. "I'll go start a pot of coffee."

"Already done." Tony tapped the top of a coffee cup she hadn't noticed. "It might be a little stronger than you like."

"The stronger the better, especially this morning." Carlita made her way into the kitchen and returned a short time later with a slice of banana bread in one hand and a cup of coffee in the other.

Rambo padded over and Carlita shook her head. "Sorry Rambo. No banana bread for you. I brought you something better." She placed a paper napkin on the table and held out a dog biscuit. "This is for you. I'll take you for a walk as soon as it's light out."

"I already took him for a walk," Tony said. "I couldn't sleep, thinking about someone wandering around down in our basement." He raised both hands over his head and stretched his back. "You think they were looking for the gems?"

"Maybe." Carlita broke off a chunk of banana bread. "I think the bones, the gems and at least one the business owners is connected. Someone on the other side of the gate was wandering around downstairs last night."

"We know for certain the Parrot House and Alder-Delaney tunnels connect," Carlita said. "I wonder if the third one, the one you weren't able to access when you snuck into the empty place across the street is connected to the Cobblestone Bed & Breakfast."

"It makes sense if they're close together." Tony rubbed the stubble on his chin. "If not, it's another business close by. Too bad we can't get inside the Cobblestone Bed & Breakfast to find out."

"We could book a night at the place," Carlita said. "Not tonight, though. We're watching Violet so you can have dinner with Shelby." She was careful to avoid using the word "date."

"True," Tony agreed. "Maybe tomorrow night. You and Mercedes could check it out."

"I was thinking the same thing while I was awake half the night. The fact Elvira found a gem inside the hollowed out space connects the gems to the woman and connects us all to the other businesses."

Tony jerked his head toward the sidewalk. "While Rambo and I were out walking this morning, I noticed a car with out-of-state license plates parked in front of the Alder-Delaney property across the street. The lights were on so sneaking back into the place is out of the question."

Carlita tilted her head and gazed toward the street. "Hmm. I have an idea. What if I bake a batch of mascarpone dark chocolate cupcakes and take them over there to welcome our new neighbors to Walton Square?"

She stood. "I'll make a few extra since I know how my Tony loves his momma's cupcakes."

Tony followed his mother into the apartment. "Ah, there's nothing like an Italian Ma to spoil her children with good food." He patted his stomach. "If I stick around here much longer, I'm gonna need to buy bigger clothes."

"I'll foot the bill." Carlita flipped the kitchen light on and lifted her apron from the hook. "I'll start on those cupcakes now. Baking always helps clear my mind."

Tony grabbed his overnight case sitting next to the sleeper sofa. "As soon as I shower, I'll head to the hardware store to pick up the stuff I'll need to wall up the tunnel."

"Thanks son." Carlita smiled. "It's so nice having you here. The only thing that could make it better was if your brother, Vinnie, was here." The smile vanished. "I sent him a text and left a voice mail on his cell phone. He still hasn't called back."

"Oh, I forgot." Tony snapped his fingers. "He called me late last night and told me he was somewheres on the Jersey Coast and he might pop in - in a week or so once he's sure no one is following him."

"Thank goodness."

Tony headed to the bathroom while Carlita assembled her baking supplies to start on the batch of cupcakes. She hummed a snappy tune as she began working. Today was already turning out to be a good day.

Once the wall was back in place, they could put the whole incident behind them and focus on making money.

Fate, however, had other plans.

Chapter 17

Mercedes wandered out of her bedroom as her mother pulled the cupcakes from the oven. "You made cupcakes for breakfast?"

"No." Carlita closed the oven door. "Tony noticed a strange car across the street with out-of-state-plates. I think it's probably our new neighbors so I decided to take a batch of mascarpone cupcakes over and introduce myself."

"And check them out," Mercedes said.

"It doesn't hurt to get to know the neighbors. This is a tight knit community." Carlita untied her apron and hung it on the hook. "I promised to go over everything you've pulled together so far and after we take a look, I say we put this thing to rest. We have enough on our plate to worry about. The shelving will be here today or tomorrow and I want to start putting the store together."

"Me too." Mercedes slipped past her mother, reached inside the kitchen cupboard and pulled out a coffee cup. "Still, aren't you at all concerned someone snuck into our basement?"

"Of course I am." Carlita shoved a fisted hand on her hip and watched her daughter pour coffee into her cup. "If I had to guess, I would say someone around here knows about the gems, that there was some sort of ring at one time and they're looking for a missing stash."

Mercedes sipped her coffee and studied her mother over the rim of the cup. "And they want them back. Do you think that just because we sealed off the tunnel they're going to give up? The gems we found are worth a small fortune."

"I suppose." Carlita's eyes slid to the gems and the wooden boxes. She'd moved the boxes next to the fireplace and they looked like decorative furniture pieces. In other words, she was hiding them in plain sight.

While the cupcakes cooled, Mercedes and Carlita headed to the dining room table to go over all of the pictures Mercedes had taken.

They started by viewing the pictures she'd taken of the skeletal remains, right before they called authorities.

Carlita slipped her reading glasses on and studied the screen. The opening where they'd discovered the bones was small. The bones were close together, as if the woman had been curled up in a fetal position. "The report said the cause of death was inconclusive."

She straightened. "I'm sure Detective Jackson figured out the tunnel leads to other areas, to other businesses nearby."

Mercedes picked up. "That means he interviewed the owner of Parrot House Restaurant and Cobblestone Bed & Breakfast." She tapped her fingernail on the top of the table.

"He may have even contacted the new…old owners of the Alder-Delaney place."

She flipped to the next picture, a shot of the dark tunnel, followed by one of the section of tunnel that was a dead end and finally a picture of the wrought iron gate. "Three businesses, all with access to the other side of the gate. Any one of them could've been involved in a smuggling ring or even murder."

"True," Carlita murmured. "We can't rule out the previous owner of this place, George Delmario. His mafia connections would make him a number one suspect. He had to have known the box of gems was in his basement."

Mercedes tucked a stray strand of hair behind her ear. "I wonder why someone didn't break into this place after Delmario's death, while it sat vacant."

"Unless…" Carlita slid out of the chair and began pacing back and forth. "They recently found out about it. We don't know the history of the Parrot House and Cobblestone Bed & Breakfast. We've already done some research on the Alder family background. Perhaps it isn't a coincidence the family purchased the property."

"There's a reason someone is wandering around in the tunnel. They're after something, even risking being caught," Mercedes said. "What if they don't stop? What if they break into our building?"

Images of a sinister figure lurking in their pawnshop, which would soon be filled with gold, gems and other valuable items, filled Carlita's head. "I hadn't considered that possibility."

Rambo pawed at the slider door and Carlita wandered over to let him out. She caught a glimpse of Tony near the back of his car. He was pulling bags of cement from the trunk.

Mercedes followed her mother out onto the patio and waved her arms at her brother. "Hey! Don't start cementing the wall yet."

Tony shifted the heavy bag of cement and frowned. "You're kiddin'."

"Nope. I'll be down in a minute to explain." Mercedes turned to her mother. "I have an idea on how we can set a trap and catch the person who's been wandering around inside our basement."

***

Tony kicked at one of the bricks with the tip of his shoe. "I got plenty of other things to keep me busy. The shelving should be here today and I can start working on that." He shot his sister a quick look. "So what's the plan?"

"Not here." Mercedes lifted her thumb in an upward motion. Mercedes, followed by Carlita and finally Tony, headed up the ladder where Tony dropped the trap door in place. "So what's the big plan?"

"My idea is to set up a sting. I watched it on this new mystery television program called 'And They Almost Got Away.' One of the main characters, a woman who was a retired private investigator, kept getting anonymous death threats. She figured it was a former client or someone she had gotten dirt on so she set up a sting to lure them out. Worked like a charm."

Mercedes turned to her mother. "You deliver your cupcakes to the new neighbors, casually mention someone has been inside your basement looking around, drop hints about the gems without coming right out and saying what it is and then tell them we're sealing the tunnel shut."

Carlita interrupted. "What about the Cobblestone Bed & Breakfast?"

"The owners of Cobblestone don't know either of us. I was thinking I could maybe book a room. After everyone settles in for the night, I'll look for the tunnel," Mercedes said.

Tony rocked back on his heels. "That's pretty good Mercedes. Sounds like you've given it some thought. In the meantime, I can start working on setting up shop."

"I'll try to get the Cobblestone B&B on the horn to make a reservation."

Carlita held up a hand. "Do you want me to go with you? I don't want you going there alone."

"No worries." Mercedes shook her head. "I already ran it by Autumn. She's going to go with me. We're going to pretend we're cousins, in town to tour the college."

"No worries?" Carlita groaned. "Now I really am worried."

"Don't be," Mercedes said. "Remember tonight is our night to watch Violet."

"Oh! I almost forgot. Maybe we should postpone it for a couple of days."

"No," Mercedes said. "Autumn and I will check into the B&B, then come back to help with Violet. We can't snoop until everyone goes to bed anyway."

The roar of a truck engine followed by a tap on the back door interrupted the conversation.

"It sounds like the delivery truck is here with our shelving." Tony greeted the delivery driver while Mercedes and Carlita headed up the steps.

Carlita paused in the outer hallway and glanced at Elvira's apartment door. "You go on inside. I'm going to stop by Elvira's place for a moment."

She lightly tapped on Elvira's apartment door. The door flew open and a disheveled Elvira appeared wearing a paint-spattered smock. A slash of lime green paint covered her right cheek.

"I hope I'm not bothering you."

"Nah! I'm working on a lampshade. It's a birthday present for my sister. She's coming for a visit in a few weeks," Elvira said.

"You have a sister?" Visions of two Elvira's swirled in Carlita's head.

"Yep. Dernice lives out in California. I haven't seen much of her since she was released from prison for armed robbery." Elvira picked at a chunk of yellow paint on her hand. "She got in with the wrong crowd but it was a rigged case. Anyhoo, she got off with a year's sentence and now she's on probation."

"Her probation officer finally issued a travel pass but she's still working on getting the charges dropped." Elvira shook her head. "I told her to stay away from those biker gangs but she wouldn't listen to me."

Elvira changed the subject. "What's up?"

"I never thought I would say this, but I need your help," Carlita said. "I would like to hire your services, investigative that is, to research the owners of three area businesses."

"Oh! A paying customer. Let me grab a form." Elvira darted back inside, returning moments later with a sheet of paper and ink pen. "I'm guessing the first one is the new/old owners across the street."

"Correct."

"Then I'm going to say the owners of the Parrot House Restaurant."

"Two for two," Carlita said. "The last one would be the owners of Cobblestone Bed & Breakfast."

Elvira stopped writing and nodded knowingly. "So you suspect one of them as the intruder and possibly the killer."

"Maybe," Carlita said. She explained to Elvira how they discovered someone was sneaking around down in their basement after hearing a shuffling and then the clink of a metal door.

"Could be the killer looking for more gems," Elvira said. "I took the one I found to Paradise Pawn and they gave me a couple grand for it." She narrowed her eyes. "I'll still have to charge you for my investigative services."

Carlita held up a hand. "I completely understand. I don't expect anyone to work for free. How long will it take for you to get back with me?"

"I could have the information to you by tomorrow morning."

"Perfect," Carlita said. "I can't wait to see what you come up with." She wandered back inside her apartment and nearly collided with Mercedes, who was hurrying around the corner.

"We're all set. Autumn and I got lucky. We got the last available room. It's called the Emperor's Suite. You should see the pictures! It looks awesome."

She gave her mother a concerned look. "I can postpone it so you and I can go instead."

Carlita, touched by her daughter's thoughtfulness, shook her head. "It's okay Mercedes. I'm not much into haunted houses. I'm sure you and Autumn will enjoy it much more. Just make sure you stay out of trouble."

"We will," Mercedes promised. "And we'll come back to help you entertain Violet, too."

"Sounds good. I'll fix a quick lunch and then we can head downstairs to help your brother assemble the shelving."

The women, along with Tony, spent the rest of the afternoon unpacking and assembling the shelves. By the time they finished, Carlita's back ached and her fingers were numb from screwing the shelves together.

It was tiring work but also rewarding as Carlita's dream of a pawnshop began to materialize.

They'd already purchased several items as they started building inventory and hit the jackpot after attending a couple estate sales. There were also several moving sales in the historic district coming up the following weekend and Carlita hoped they would be as successful with the moving sales as they had been with the estate sales.

According to Tony, he'd gotten several calls the previous evening and that morning from people interested in making a quick buck. He'd scheduled some appointments for later that afternoon, which would give them enough time to clean up their mess.

The first prospective seller arrived as Carlita carried the last empty shipping box from the shop. "Good luck," she told her son before heading to the alley and the dumpster out back.

Mercedes beat her to the shower and she emerged a short time later. "Autumn will be here shortly and then we're going to head over to Cobblestone to check in."

Carlita waited for Autumn and Mercedes to leave before she wandered into the bathroom. Tony would need to shower before he picked up Shelby for their non-date. She hadn't had much time to think of ways to entertain Violet but figured the least they could do was frost some of the cupcakes still sitting on the counter and maybe even take Rambo to the park.

The bathroom was like a revolving door as Carlita exited and Tony headed in. He seemed nervous as he emerged from the shower wearing a pair of black dress slacks and blue polo shirt. His hair, still wet from the shower, was slicked back. "Do you think this is good enough for a swanky restaurant?"

"Where are you taking her?" Carlita set the e-reader she'd been reading on her lap.

"It's called Seventy-Fifth. Nouveau cuisine, whatever that is."

"Nouvelle cuisine," Carlita said. "From what I've heard, it's fancy French food. The focus is more on presentation than substance. Maybe you should eat a sandwich before you go."

"Nah. I'll be okay." Tony slipped his shoes on and smoothed a lock of wayward hair in place.

"You look handsome as all get out." Carlita impulsively jumped out of her chair and hugged her son. His cologne smelled familiar. It was a scent her Vinnie had often worn and reminded her of a combination of leather and the outdoors.

"You smell and look like your father." Carlita blinked back sudden tears and forced a smile. "I hope Shelby and you have a wonderful time. Don't forget to bring Violet over on your way out."

Tony wrapped an arm around his mother's shoulders. He knew there were times it was still hard on his mother. Despite all of Vincent Garlucci's faults, he had been a good father, a good husband and his passing had left a huge gap in all of their lives. "I will and thanks for everything." He didn't wait for a reply as he strode out of the apartment.

A lone tear trickled down Carlita's cheek. She hadn't meant to get so emotional but the sight of her son, the spitting image of his father, had reached down and squeezed her heart.

She quietly closed the door behind him.

Chapter 18

"I'm going to put lots and lots of frosting on this cupcake. Chocolate frosting is Mommy's favorite." Violet loaded her knife with frosting and stuck a big glob on the side of the cupcake.

"She's going to love it," Carlita assured the young girl. "You might need a little more frosting on this other side." She pointed to a part of the cupcake without frosting.

"Uh-huh." Violet scrunched her eyebrows as she concentrated on her masterpiece. She scooped even more frosting from the bowl and smeared it on an empty spot. "There!"

Carlita grinned at the cupcake and patted Violet's head. "Perfect. Let's put it back here so we don't mix it up with the others and then you can start on yours."

Carlita listened as Violet chattered about school, her friend, Melody, and her teacher. When they finished, Carlita dragged a chair to the sink because Violet insisted she help with dishes.

She dropped an apron over Violet's head to keep her pink dress clean and then handed her a soap-filled sponge. "My mommy lets me help all the time. She said if I'm good she's going to get me a kitty for my birthday."

"When is your birthday?"

"Junelie something." Violet stopped scrubbing as she tried to remember the exact date. "Daddy won't be here for my birthday."

Carlita paused. "Does your daddy live close by?"

Violet shrugged. "I don't know. He left after he hit mommy and she had to go to the hospital. I had to stay with grampies until mommy got better."

"Then we moved here." Violet picked up her frosted knife and rubbed the sponge across the side. "I'm going to name my kitty Elsa. My favorite movie is *Frozen*."

"What a pretty name," Carlita said. *Poor Shelby. Poor Violet. No wonder Shelby didn't want her name on the outside of the building.* Carlita wondered if the ex was searching for Shelby and their daughter.

Carlita and Violet finished cleaning the dirty dishes. Violet hopped off the chair and darted across the kitchen floor to hug Rambo. "Can we go for a walk now?"

It would be dark soon. Carlita glanced out the slider. If they planned to walk to the park, they needed to get a move on. "Yes. We'll go now."

She helped Violet slip the apron off and her sweater on and then hooked Rambo's collar to his leash. They made their way out of the building and onto the sidewalk where they ran into Mercedes and Autumn, who were racing down the sidewalk on their Segways.

"We better jump out of the way," Carlita told Violet as they stepped to the edge of the sidewalk and waited for the women to stop.

"Sorry we're late," Autumn said. "The owner gave us a tour of the bed and breakfast."

"Did you see the basement?" Carlita asked.

"No." Mercedes' shoulders slumped. "We toured all the upstairs common areas and all of the living areas downstairs. We only got a quick glimpse of the kitchen so we're thinking it might be in that area of the house."

"We're going to check it out later." Autumn winked at Carlita and then hopped off her Segway. "Hello Violet. Do you remember me?"

Violet hid behind Carlita and shook her head.

"She's the one who found Grayvie and brought him to our house to live with us," Carlita explained.

"Grayvie likes to play with me," Violet said. "We're going to the park."

"We'll go with you. Would you like a ride?" Mercedes asked.

"Yes!" Violet hopped up and down on one foot.

"No!" Carlita shook her head firmly. Violet pouted until becoming distracted by *A Scoop in Time Ice Cream* shop.

"Can we have ice cream?" Violet asked.

"We just ate a cupcake. Let me think about it," Carlita said.

The park was crowded with bikers, walkers and joggers. There were even a few strollers. The cool evening air reminded Carlita that fall was right around the corner and she could hardly wait.

Rambo made his rounds as he visited some of his favorite spots. Violet was thrilled to follow the pooch and they made a game out of chasing one another across the meticulously manicured park lawn.

Mercedes and Autumn also kept the young girl busy…inspecting the nearby flower gardens and the statue of the waving girl. Finally, when the street lamps started to flicker, Carlita slid off the park bench. "We need to get back before dark."

The walk home was at a more leisurely pace and when they got to the ice cream shop, Carlita decided it wouldn't hurt if Violet had one teensy kiddie cone.

The cupcake she'd sampled earlier had been plenty for Carlita so she passed on ice cream. Mercedes and Autumn both ordered double scoop cones and after paying for the cones, the four of them crossed the street and headed to their courtyard.

A faint light shone through the window of the Alder-Delaney place and Carlita briefly wondered how Elvira's research was progressing.

After they finished eating their ice cream, Autumn and Mercedes climbed onto their Segways for the ride back to the Cobblestone Bed & Breakfast while Violet, Rambo and Carlita walked back to the apartment.

They had just settled in on the living room sofa to watch Violet's favorite movie when the door opened and Tony stepped inside. He was alone.

Carlita shifted on the couch. "Back so soon?"

"Back so soon? We were gone for hours," Tony said.

"The evening flew by, didn't it Violet?"

"Yep." Violet nodded solemnly. "Can I come back again sometime?"

"Absolutely!" Carlita gave her a quick hug. "We can bake cookies next time. Which reminds me. Don't forget your mom's cupcake and your extra one."

They had carefully placed the frosted cupcakes on a paper plate and then covered them with a loose layer of plastic wrap.

Carlita helped Violet carry them across the hall to her apartment. The door was ajar.

"Knock! Knock!"

A beaming Shelby appeared. "I was going to come over but Tony said he would let you know we were home." She knelt down and hugged her daughter. "Did you have fun?"

Violet nodded. "Yep. We frosted cupcakes. I played with Grayvie and Rambo and then we went to the park and ate ice cream."

Carlita chuckled. "I hope I didn't overdo it on the sweets. It was a small cone."

Shelby stood. "Don't worry about it. It sounds like you had lots of fun."

Violet took the plate of cupcakes from Carlita and held them out to her mother. "I made this one for you." She pointed at one of the lopsided frosted cupcakes.

"It looks yummy. I can't wait to try it."

"I'm going to watch my movie now." Violet handed the plate of cupcakes to her mother. She lunged forward and wrapped both arms around Carlita's legs. "Thank you for letting me come over and play."

For the second time that day, Carlita blinked back sudden tears. "You're welcome." She bent down and kissed the top of Violet's head. "We'll do it again real soon," she promised.

Violet released her grip and skipped to the living room.

"Thank you for watching her." Shelby smiled gratefully as she watched her young daughter hop onto the couch.

Carlita reached out and touched her arm. "Thank you for letting me enjoy being a grandmother again, at least for a little while. We had a ball."

She impulsively hugged the young mother and then let herself out of the apartment. The evening had been one of the best Carlita had had in a long time.

When she stepped inside her apartment, Carlita spotted Tony sitting out on the deck. She wandered across the living room to join him. "It's a beautiful evening."

Tony turned. "Yes, it is. Thanks for watching Violet. She's a character."

"She sure is," Carlita agreed. "Spending time with her makes me miss Gracie, Noel and little Paulie." The three belonged to Carlita's youngest son, Paulie, and his wife, Gina, who lived in Clifton Falls, New York.

She changed the subject. "I don't mean to pry but how was the date, uh, I mean dinner?"

Tony smiled. "You are prying."

"I know, but I'm your mother and mothers get to ask those kinds of questions."

"It was good." Tony shifted his gaze and stared into the alley. "We really hit it off. Shelby is different, more laid back. It's hard to describe."

Carlita smiled knowingly. "She exudes a charm…Southern Charm. The girls up north are brassy and sassy." She shrugged. "For some, Shelby would be too nice, too sweet, if that makes sense."

"Yeah." Tony nodded. "Not me. I like it."

"Are you going to ask her out again, I mean for a non-date?"

"See? Now you are prying," Tony joked. "Yeah," he added softly. "But next time, I'm going to ask her out on a date, both her and Violet."

"So I guess you're going to stay in Savannah," Carlita replied in the same soft voice her son had used.

"Yeah." Tony nodded. "I guess I am."

Chapter 19

Autumn pulled her orange knit shirt over her head and tossed it on the bed.

"What are you doing?" Mercedes asked.

"Changing." Autumn reached inside her overnight bag and pulled out a black shirt. "Bright orange is gonna stick out like a sore thumb if we're trying to remain stealth and snoop."

"I never thought about that." Mercedes tugged on the corner of her hot pink cotton blouse.

"I figured as much." Autumn reached inside her bag a second time, pulled out an identical black blouse and tossed it to her friend. "I've got you covered."

"Literally," Mercedes joked. She glanced at the clock on the fireplace mantle: 11:45 p.m. "How much longer?"

"Only a few more minutes. I want to check my gear one last time." Autumn reached inside her backpack. "Stun gun, flashlight, baby oil, duct tape, cell phone."

"Why in the world would we need baby oil?"

"I dunno. I saw it on a show one time. They squirted baby oil on rusty metal hinges to stop them from squeaking. It might come in handy for the trap door."

"Huh." Mercedes shrugged. It made sense, in a weird way.

"Based on the layout of this house, I was thinking the trap door is probably in the kitchen."

"If we get caught, we could say we were looking for a glass of water," Mercedes said.

Autumn tapped the side of her forehead. "Great minds think alike. I was thinking the same thing." She shoved her cell phone in her right hand back pocket and the flashlight in the opposite pocket. She handed the duct tape and baby oil to Mercedes.

"What do you want me to do with these?"

"Hang onto them." Autumn led the way as the women tiptoed into the hall. Thankfully, their room was next to the staircase that led to the first floor. The house was well over a century old and every stair tread Mercedes stepped on creaked.

"Shh." Autumn held a finger to her lips.

"You shush!" Mercedes shot back. "I can't help it the stairs squeak."

When they reached the bottom, Autumn abruptly stopped.

Mercedes, distracted by the tick-tock of the grandfather clock at the bottom of the stairs, didn't realize Autumn had stopped and crashed into her.

Both girls lunged forward.

Mercedes arms flailed wildly in a desperate attempt to avoid toppling over. She grabbed the newel post and hung on for dear life.

Autumn stumbled forward and fell head first into a silk ficus tree in the corner. The tree tilted precariously and came to rest against the decorative drapes that separated the hall and the paneled library.

"Sorry," Mercedes said. "I didn't see you stop."

"I'm no worse for the wear." Autumn shifted the tree to an upright position. "Neither is the plant. Let's keep moving."

The girls crept down the hall and turned right when they reached the end. They stepped into the dining room.

"Whoops! Little miscalculation," Autumn said. "I guess we need to go left." She backtracked and pushed a swinging door open as they stepped into the kitchen.

The light from an outside street lamp illuminated the quartz counters and large stainless steel farmhouse sink.

Autumn pulled her flashlight from her pocket and switched it on.

"If our excuse is coming down here for a glass of water, why would we need a flashlight?" Mercedes asked.

"Good point." Autumn turned the flashlight off and felt along the wall. The kitchen lights flickered and bright light illuminated the kitchen.

"I love this kitchen." Mercedes ran her hand across the countertop. "I bet Mom would love it too."

The fronts of several of the kitchen cabinets were clear glass and Mercedes spotted a cupboard filled with drink glasses. "Over there."

Autumn reached inside the cabinet and pulled out two glasses. She walked over to the sink and filled both glasses with water before taking a sip. "Let's start looking." She carried her drink glass as she circled the room.

Mercedes stopped in front of what appeared to be a corner closet. "I wonder what's in here." She opened the door and stuck her head inside. It was a pantry.

The pantry was large. Canned goods, boxes of cereal, loaves of bread and other staples lined the shelves.

"It's the pantry." Mercedes started to close the door when something caught her eye. It was a large, square cutout, smack dab in the center of the pantry floor. "Bingo!"

"You found it?" Autumn set her glass on the counter and hurried over.

"Yeah, and it's unlocked." Mercedes dropped to her knees and inspected the round ring near one end of the cutout. "This one looks a lot like ours except it's a different color." She grabbed the ring and gave it a light tug. It lifted ever so slightly so she tugged harder.

The trap door silently lifted and she pushed it back. "Cool. This one has hinges."

With the door safely out of the way, Autumn turned her flashlight on and shined the light into the dark opening. "I see a set of stairs." She took a tentative step down while Mercedes hung back.

"Well? Are you coming with?"

"I don't think we should go down there. We know it exists. If you take a quick glimpse inside, you can see if there's a tunnel and the direction it leads," Mercedes said.

"Don't tell me you're afraid of a tunnel." Autumn took another step down.

"I'm not. It's just that..."

"Can I help you find something?" The inn's owner, Bonnie Aberdeen, appeared in the doorway.

Chapter 20

Mercedes grabbed the railing and spun around.

Autumn hurried up the steps, flashlight in hand. "We came down for a drink of water and could've sworn we heard a noise coming from the pantry so we thought we would check it out."

"And you happened to have a flashlight with you?" The woman pointed at the light Autumn was holding.

"We heard this place was haunted," Mercedes said.

"We were hoping we might see a ghost," Autumn added.

Bonnie Aberdeen narrowed her gaze. "So the plan was to find a ghost and then what? Slime them with baby oil and wrap them in duct tape?"

She pointed at the baby oil and duct tape sticking out of Mercedes' back pockets.

"Haha." Mercedes tapped her pockets. "When you put it like that, it does seem kind of silly."

The woman eased past Mercedes. "The basement is off limits, ghost or not."

"No problem." Autumn scurried up the rest of the steps and hurried out of the pantry. Mercedes was right behind her. "I blame it on my ECD. Excessive compulsive disorder. I act first and think later."

Bonnie closed the trap door and flipped the lock in place before turning off the pantry light and closing the door. "It appears your cousin does, too."

The property owner watched them like a hawk as they refilled their water glasses and headed down the hall.

Mercedes could feel the woman's eyes bore into her back as they wandered to the bottom of the stairs and started back up.

Autumn and Mercedes remained silent until they reached their room and Autumn closed the door behind them.

"That was a close call." Mercedes set her glass of water on the bedside stand. "At least we know she's not a killer. She could have easily stabbed or shot us and buried our bodies in the basement."

"Our families would come search for us," Autumn said confidently.

"By the time they found out, it would be too late." Mercedes flopped on the bed and flung a hand over her eyes. "Another failed mission."

"Not quite," Autumn said. "Before Mrs. Aberdeen caught us, I was able to take a peek downstairs. There's definitely a tunnel and if my sense of direction is correct, it leads right to the Parrot House Restaurant, which means it connects to the other tunnels, including your place and the Alder-Delaney property."

The girls took turns in the bathroom getting ready for bed. Thankfully, the bed was large and they had plenty of room to spread out.

Sleep eluded Mercedes, who was convinced Bonnie Aberdeen would sneak into their room at any moment and strangle them while they slept.

Autumn, on the other hand, quickly fell asleep. Her soft snores from the other side of the bed also kept Mercedes awake. While she lay there unable to sleep, Mercedes came up with a plan to add Bonnie Aberdeen to their sting. She wondered why she hadn't thought of it before.

When morning came, the girls wandered down to the dining room. Other overnight guests were already seated at the tables, enjoying a leisurely breakfast. There were several small food stations including a coffee and juice station, a pancake station and a meat station.

The smell of frying bacon and a whiff of peaches caused Mercedes' stomach to growl. "Something smells delicious." She wandered over to a man, standing behind one of the stations. He was cooking the Cobblestone's signature dish - French toast stuffed with cream cheese and a dash of pureed Georgia peaches.

Thankfully, Bonnie Aberdeen was nowhere in sight as the women filled their plates with food and settled in at a table for two near one of the windows.

Autumn and Mercedes kept their conversation light as they discussed the property as well as historic Savannah. After they finished eating, Autumn suggested touring the grounds.

Mercedes patted her stomach. "I'm so full, I'll waddle around."

"It'll be good exercise."

"You're right." Mercedes dabbed the corners of her mouth with her napkin, placed it on the edge of her plate and slid out of her chair.

They zigzagged past the tables, out of the dining room and exited through the front door.

The air was heavy with morning dew and Mercedes sucked in a deep breath. She could smell the Savannah River, not far from the bed and breakfast.

"Let's head to the garden first." Autumn wandered down the steps and turned onto the meandering path that led to the side of the house. "Based on my calculations, the tunnel would start somewhere over here." She pointed to the small porch near the back of the stately home. "It took a small turn so it went that away."

Mercedes shaded her eyes and studied the sidewalk. "So you think it connects from there to the Parrot House. Beyond that is the Alder-Delaney property. Our place is a little farther down and to the left."

"Correct."

"I came up with a great plan while I was wide awake last night," Mercedes said. "Now that we know the tunnels connect, we need to add Bonnie Aberdeen to our list of possible suspects."

They finished their tour of the grounds and Mercedes explained how they could include Cobblestone without raising any suspicion as to the motive.

"Brilliant," Autumn said. "Why didn't I think of that?"

"Because you were sound asleep," Mercedes joked. "Now all we have to do is make sure my mom is on board."

They wandered back to their room to pack. Mercedes was sad to leave the beautiful home. She tossed Autumn her black shirt. "Thanks for the loan."

She folded her shorts and shoved them in the corner of her overnight bag. "This was so much fun. Maybe we could start scoping out more of the area bed and breakfasts."

"I would love to," Autumn said. "I've toured a few, mostly the ones rumored to be haunted but I've never spent the night in one until last night. There's a bunch of them in Savannah."

The girls finished packing their bags and as they exited their suite, Mercedes took one last wistful glance around the room.

They found Bonnie Aberdeen inside the sunroom and told her how much they'd enjoyed staying at the bed and breakfast. The owner didn't mention the incident from the previous night and told the girls to come back anytime. "Don't forget your Segways. The shed door is unlocked."

Mrs. Aberdeen had offered to let them store their Segways inside the shed and Mercedes and Autumn thanked her before heading outside and to the back of the property.

Mercedes eased the shed door open and stepped inside. She looped the handle of her overnight bag on the handle of the Segway and reached for her helmet. "Check out all the cool stuff in here the Aberdeens aren't even using." The shelves were crammed full of miscellaneous items including an old metal tricycle, white wicker planters and a stack of brightly colored chair cushions. "I bet we could sell some of this stuff in the pawnshop."

The girls steered their Segways out of the shed, careful to close the door and secure the latch behind them before they climbed on them for the short trip to Mercedes' place.

When they reached the apartment, Mercedes hopped off her Segway. "Thanks for joining me on the spy mission. I'm sorry we weren't able to crack the case."

Autumn waved a hand. "Nah! I had fun. The only thing that would've made it better is if we could've explored the tunnel." She glanced at her watch. "I better get going. I'm gonna stop by to say hi to Steve before heading to work."

Mercedes waved good-bye to her friend before steering her Segway into the alley and parking it next to the back door. She removed her helmet and placed it on the handle before grabbing her overnight bag and making her way inside where she found her mother and Tony sorting through packing boxes.

Carlita lowered the power tool she was holding and turned to her daughter. "Well?"

"We need to add Bonnie Aberdeen to our sting operation." Mercedes told her mother how they had snuck into the pantry and located the trap door. "Autumn said the basement connected to a tunnel."

"Did you explore the tunnel?" Tony asked.

"Nope. We got busted snooping around by the property owner." Mercedes swiped her hand across her brow. "It was a close call. We told the owner, Mrs. Aberdeen, we heard a noise and since the place was rumored to be haunted, we hoped to spot a ghost."

"And she bought the story?"

"I dunno. When we told her good-bye this morning, she didn't mention it. We briefly met Mr. Aberdeen yesterday but never saw him again," Mercedes said. "Mrs. Aberdeen let Autumn and me store our Segways in their shed. The place is full of antiques and stuff."

"My gut tells me someone in Walton Square is hiding something," Mercedes said. "Here's my theory. George Delmario double-crossed his partners, some of the other Walton Square business owners. He hid the gems in his basement, walled off the tunnel and then started selling them on the black market."

She continued. "The partners/smugglers got into some sort of argument when one of the partners figured out Delmario had double-crossed them and they killed him."

"Say you're right," Carlita said. "It still doesn't explain whose skeletal remains we found hidden in the wall."

"Delmario was no saint," Tony said. "Not if he was related to Frank Delmario. He could've killed someone and hidden the body in the wall."

"I asked Elvira to do some preliminary research on the history of the properties connected to our tunnel," Carlita said.

"You asked Elvira to snoop for us?" Mercedes asked.

"I figured we could help her out and she could help us out," Carlita said. "Speaking of helping, your brother and I could use a hand sorting through the goods."

"Let me change. I'll be right back." Mercedes headed upstairs to change and to drop off her overnight bag.

When she returned, the trio made quick work of sorting through the boxes. Tony told them he'd been slammed with calls from the online ads Mercedes had placed and had a slew of appointments later that afternoon.

Carlita hung an antique clock on the wall behind the jewelry counter. "You're doing a good job, son, picking out merchandise and I'm thrilled that you're going to move here."

Mercedes nearly dropped the box of baseball cards she was inspecting. "You're staying? For real?" A slow smile spread across her face. "So your non-date with Shelby went well?"

Tony grinned at his sister. "Yeah. She's a real sweetheart and little Violet? She's one of the cutest kids I've ever met. Smart as a whip, too, but that's not the only reason."

Tony set the wristwatch he was holding onto the display case. "I mean, we hardly know each other. It's just." He glanced around the room. "I can't walk away and leave you two to run the pawnshop by yourselves. You need a third wheel, another business partner. Maybe I'm ready to become an honest businessman, ready to turn over a new leaf and all."

He continued. "I was thinkin' though. I don't wanna move into the upstairs apartment. There's plenty of room to add a studio apartment right here behind the pawnshop. We can hire your contractor to fix it up so it has everything I need. That way, I can keep an eye on the business and we can rent the upper unit for cash flow."

"Are you sure?" Carlita asked. "I'd hate for you to feel like you have to settle."

"I'm positive. I'd rather be down here where I can keep a close eye on things."

Carlita darted around the counter and hugged her son. "I'll call Bob Lowman this morning and have him get started."

"Remember, I gotta go back home and wrap up some loose ends, sell my condo and pack my things," Tony said.

"I figured by this morning you would've changed your mind." Carlita clasped her hands together. "You go ahead and take care of everything up north and by the time you get back down here, Bob will have your apartment ready to go."

Carlita hugged her son one last time and she nearly floated up the stairs to call her contractor. She was finally making progress in keeping her promise to her husband, Vinnie, to get their children out of the mafia!

Chapter 21

Carlita left Bob a message and then headed across the hall to Elvira's apartment. Elvira didn't answer when Carlita knocked and she guessed her tenant had already left for her job at the Savannah Architectural Society.

Mercedes, who had followed her mother upstairs, met her in the hall. "Tony is meeting with some sellers so I thought I'd come up here to go over the plan to oust whoever is sneaking around downstairs. We need to include the new/old owners of Alder-Delaney place, the owner of Parrot House Restaurant and Bonnie Aberdeen, the proprietor of Cobblestone Bed and Breakfast. Since I've already met Bonnie, I think you should approach her."

"What's the plan?" Carlita asked as she opened their apartment door.

"You deliver the cupcakes to the new owners across the street, welcoming them to the neighborhood. As for Pirate Pete and Bonnie, you can take one of those handy dandy business cards we had printed and tell them you're in the market for items to sell in our pawnshop. Give them one of our cards and then casually start a conversation about your concerns someone is sneaking into our basement. You can mention you're concerned whoever it is - is after items we found in the basement so you're going to have your son seal off the tunnel tomorrow."

"You think I should tell them about the gems?"

"No," Mercedes shook her head. "Just hint around that we found something. If you give them a deadline, which is sealing off the tunnel tomorrow, it will force the culprit into making another appearance tonight."

She continued. "In the meantime, I'll work on setting a trap."

"This sounds dangerous," Carlita fretted.

"Not at all. We're going to hide a small camera in the corner of the basement with a bird's eye view of the tunnel. I'll track down a camera today since you'll be busy laying the groundwork."

Carlita still wasn't convinced the whole thing wasn't going to backfire on them but she didn't have much of a choice. Someone was lurking below ground. The fact that Tony planned to move in behind the pawnshop was even more motivation to uncover the culprit. Desperate people committed desperate crimes.

Carlita's cell phone chirped. It was Bob Lowman. She answered the phone and briefly explained what they needed to have done. Bob promised he would stop by the following day to go over the renovations with Tony.

She had no more hung up the phone when she heard a knock on the door. Carlita hurried to the door and peeked through the peephole. It was Elvira.

Carlita swung the door open and stepped to the side. "I can't wait to hear what you found out."

"Boy! I hope we're not stirring up a hornet's nest." Elvira waved the loose stack of papers she was holding. "This neighborhood was a hotbed of illegal activity and it appears this place right here was the hub."

Elvira didn't wait for an invitation as she made her way to the dining room table. She plopped down in one of the chairs and spread the papers out on the table.

Mercedes, who had disappeared inside her bedroom, joined them.

"Let's start with the illustrious previous owner of your property," Elvira said as she slipped her reading glasses on. "His name was George Delmario. Mr. Delmario had numerous brushes with the local law enforcement. He was under investigation several times for extortion, racketeering and money laundering. Last but not least, he was charged with illegal transportation of goods across state lines…oh, and tax evasion."

Elvira tapped the top of the paper with her finger. "If I didn't know better, I'd say this fella was in with the mob."

Mercedes coughed and began to pound her chest. "Swallowed wrong," she gasped.

Carlita thumped her daughter's leg under the table.

"Ouch." Mercedes glared at her mother.

"Are you all right dear? Perhaps you need to go get a drink of water." Carlita smiled sweetly.

"I'm fine." Mercedes frowned.

Elvira shot them both a puzzled glance before she flipped to the second sheet. "Next in line is James Alder, who moved here from England. From what I could uncover, he was a sea merchant. Two of his wives died under mysterious circumstances back in England. He met and married his third wife, Mary Beth

Delaney, the wealthy daughter of shipping magnet Horace Delaney, after moving to Savannah.

They had two children together, Bridget and John. Mary Beth vanished when the children were school age, never to be seen again. James stayed on, living in the house across the street that he built for Mary Beth. The children grew up and moved away. As far as I can tell, they never returned.

Elvira rattled the papers. "Reading between the lines, I think the children suspected their father somehow did away with their mother. James Alder died alone in the house. In fact, news reports say he died of natural causes but it took several days before neighbors reported smelling a foul odor coming from the place and police found his body inside."

Mercedes interrupted. "I wonder if the skeletal remains belonged to Mary Beth Alder.

James, a serial killer, murdered her and hid her body behind the wall."

"He would be suspect #1 in my book," Elvira said. "Perhaps his children are picking up where he left off. You know the saying - the apple doesn't fall very far from the tree."

"Course that's not to say your predecessor here wasn't without blood on his hands." Elvira leaned in and studied Carlita's face. "How did you say you came to own this chunk of real estate?"

"I inherited it from my husband," Carlita mumbled. "So what did you find out about Pirate Pete Taylor?"

"Peter D. Taylor." Elvira shuffled the papers. "He's another interesting character with a colorful history. The Parrot House Restaurant has been in his family for generations, since the mid-1700's when Pete's ancestors, seamen by trade, pirates by legend, built the place. The Taylors initially opened the Parrot House as an inn for seafarers. It evolved into a hangout for some of the most notorious pirates on the high seas."

"According to what I could dig up, they were a scary bunch, pirating on the high seas, taking over other ships by force and stealing whatever they could. Rumor has it they buried some of the booty on Tybee Island, not far from here. We should go check it out," Elvira said.

"Maybe later, after we figure out who's lurking around in the tunnels," Carlita answered noncommittally. *No way was she going to jump onto that train!*

Elvira lifted the sheet and squinted her eyes. "The Taylors owned not only the Parrot House but also the building adjacent to their property. Cobblestone..."

"Bed and Breakfast," Carlita and Mercedes finished Elvira's sentence.

"Imagine that," Mercedes murmured.

"You didn't ask me to research the Cobblestone but I did a little digging around anyway, free of charge of course," Elvira said. She lifted the piece of paper on the bottom of the stack. "There wasn't much to go on. The owners, the Aberdeens, bought the place earlier this year. The property had changed hands several times over the past few years. The previous owners, an elderly couple, decided to sell out and buy a condo on the river. The new owners are in the process of a complete renovation."

"How long ago?" Carlita asked.

"Six months. The paper ran a lengthy story about it," Elvira said. "The place is full of history, what with it at one time being linked to the Parrot House. It appears the new owners sank a small fortune into remodeling the place."

"It's gorgeous," Mercedes confirmed. "My friend, Autumn, and I stayed there last night. The place is huge and they have some magnificent gardens. They're still working on it and it looks as if they're putting in a pool." She shifted her gaze to her mother. "If we ever get tired of running a retail business, we could turn the place next door into a B&B."

Carlita frowned. "What about my restaurant, Ravello?"

"Ravello? You already picked a name?" Mercedes asked.

"Ravello is the name of the town where your father was born. It's not far from Amalfi's coast. Your father took me there years ago, to meet his grandparents. It was a picturesque village." Carlita smiled. "I thought it would be a fitting tribute to our Italian heritage."

"I love the idea." Mercedes squeezed her mother's hand. "We'll talk about it later."

"I love Italian food." Elvira licked her lips. "Anyhoo. That's about all I've got for now."

"Thank you, Elvira." Carlita stood. "How much do I owe you?"

Elvira straightened the papers and cleared her throat. "I didn't use my skip trace software so I won't charge you for that, but I did more than a basic search. Sixty bucks for all four searches?"

"You went above and beyond what I asked." Carlita reached for her purse on the counter, pulled out four twenty-dollar bills and handed the cash to her tenant. I'm giving you a little extra and won't even claim this as a business expense. Consider it a gift."

"Thanks!" Elvira folded the bills and shoved them in her front pocket before handing the papers to Carlita. "These are yours to keep. Let me know if you need anything else."

Carlita led her to the front door.

"Let me know when you're ready to head over to Tybee Island to start kicking some sand around. I'd love to scope it out."

"I'll keep that in mind." She held the door and waited until Elvira was in the hall before closing it behind her. "Elvira's information was helpful."

"It sure was." Mercedes crossed her arms and leaned back in the chair. "I guess I better get a move on and start hunting down a surveillance camera while you make your neighborhood rounds."

Chapter 22

Carlita juggled the tin of cupcakes in one hand and pressed the doorbell. She took a quick glance behind her at the car, hoping it belonged to the new owner and that she wasn't wasting her time.

The door abruptly swung open and a tall thin man peered down at her. "Yes?"

"Hello. I-uh. I'm Carlita Garlucci, your new neighbor. I thought I would drop by and welcome you to the neighborhood with a batch of homemade mascarpone cupcakes." She held out the tin of cupcakes. "We're excited to have new neighbors here in Walton Square."

"What a nice gesture." The man took the tin. "Thank you." He started to close the door.

Carlita wedged her foot in the opening. "I didn't catch your name."

"John. John Alder." The man opened the door a little wider and his expression grew grim. "Listen. I'm sure you've heard all about my family and me so you can lay off the Welcome Wagon act. You're here to sniff around and find out if my family is as evil and awful as the rumors purport us to be."

Carlita hung her head. "You're partially right, on the snooping part but not the other." She lifted her gaze and looked him squarely in the eye. "We all have our share of ghosts in the closet and I'm no exception. I honestly did want to welcome you to the neighborhood. Whether you choose to believe it or not is entirely up to you."

She pointed at her building. "My children and I are opening a pawnshop so if you have anything you're considering selling, we might be interested in buying it."

Carlita, still a little hot under the collar at his verbal attack, turned to go. "I'm sure the investigators stopped by to tell you about the skeletal remains found near our basement. My children and I found something else in our basement and since we're being honest with each other, I'll tell you someone is snooping around *my* property and I intend to put a stop to it pronto by sealing the tunnel tomorrow."

Carlita stomped off. She was still trembling when she reached the corner and crossed the street. It was obvious John Alder was an angry, defensive man with a chip on his shoulder but he didn't have to take it out on her!

She slowed her pace as she entered the park and then settled onto a bench facing the river.

After she calmed, Carlita made her way inside the Parrot House Restaurant and to the hostess station just inside the front door. "Yes. I would like to have a word with Pirate Pete. I'm his neighbor, Carlita Garlucci. We met a few days ago."

"I'll see if I can track Pete down." The woman disappeared into the back and returned a short time later, followed by Pirate Pete Taylor.

A broad smile crossed his face. "Mrs. Garlucci. It's so nice to see you again. Are you here for lunch?"

"No, but now that you mention it, perhaps my children and I should make plans to stop by for dinner. Do you take reservations?"

Pete nodded. "We do but you come back anytime we're open and we'll find a spot for you and your family." He changed the subject. "How can I help you?"

Carlita pulled a pawnshop business card from her purse and handed it to Pete. "My children and I will be opening our pawnshop soon and we are still in the market for merchandise. Naturally, I thought of this place, what with all the history. If you're looking to clean out your closets or attic, we would love to take a look at anything you're willing to part with."

Pete shot her a quick glance, studied the card and slid it into his front shirt pocket. "We try to go through our inventory at least once a year and usually donate to charity for auction but I'll be sure to keep you in mind. We should start cleaning for end of year inventory in the next month or so."

"Thank you. I'd be interested in whatever you might want to get rid of." Carlita would love to get her hands on some real pirate booty. "My children and I found some interesting stuff boxed up in our basement. There was also a tunnel, similar to the one you showed my son and me the other day, except ours was sealed shut so my son, curious to find out what was behind it, broke through. We found skeletal remains behind a hollowed out wall." She shivered. "The local authorities have wrapped up their investigation so Tony, my son, is going to seal it shut tomorrow."

"I heard about the body," Pete said. "An investigator, can't remember his name now, stopped by to ask a few questions." The hostess approached Pete. "We have a guest complaint at table twenty-two."

Carlita said her good-byes, promising to stop back that evening or the following evening for dinner. She stepped out onto the sidewalk and headed toward Cobblestone Bed & Breakfast, her third and final stop.

She slowed as she studied the elegant exterior. On one side was a meandering path that led to an intricately detailed cast iron portico. An expansive covered porch graced the front entrance. Spindle rails and gable trim pieces gave the place an air of old world charm.

Carlita had begun studying some of Savannah's historic architecture after attending an afternoon tea at her friend, Glenda Fox's, stately manor.

This home was a stunning example of a gothic revival. It sported oriel windows, a form of rounded bay windows, on both the upper and lower level of the two-story home.

She made her way up the steps to the dark mahogany double door. The lower half of the door was solid wood. The top was a frosted glass pattern with an intricate scrollwork design on both sides.

Carlita gingerly rang the doorbell and Westminster chimes echoed from within.

The door opened and a slight woman dressed in a dark uniform stood on the other side, a puzzled look on her face. "Did you lose your key?"

"Oh!" Carlita's hand flew to her mouth. "I forgot this is a bed and breakfast."

"Yes." The woman smiled. "Please come in."

Carlita followed the woman into the large foyer. On one side was an enormous marble fireplace. On the other, an elegant curved staircase. A three-tiered teardrop crystal chandelier caught her eye. "This home is gorgeous," Carlita whispered.

"Yes ma'am. The owners have worked hard restoring the property." She stopped abruptly. "Are you here to make a reservation?"

"No. I'm an area business owner and was wondering if I could speak to one of the owners."

"Of course. Mrs. Aberdeen is in the kitchen. I'll go get her."

The woman disappeared down the long hall, the sharp click of her heels echoing on the gleaming oak floor. Carlita shifted to the center of the foyer, afraid to get too close to the antiques displayed inside a nearby curio cabinet.

"May I help you?"

Carlita shifted her gaze and smiled as a woman approached. "Mrs. Aberdeen?"

"Yes." The woman held out a hand. "Tia said you were an area business owner. I'm Bonnie Aberdeen, co-owner of Cobblestone Bed & Breakfast."

Carlita shook the woman's hand. "Carlita Garlucci. I own some apartments over on Mulberry Street. My children and I will be opening a…she almost didn't want to say the word 'pawnshop,' fearing that a woman with a home this magnificent wouldn't appreciate having a pawnshop in her neighborhood. "…a pawnshop. High end, of course." She hurried on. "I heard you recently renovated this entire property and I have to say it's stunning."

"Thank you." Bonnie gazed around. "It has been a lot of hard work."

"You've done an amazing job," Carlita continued. "We're still looking for merchandise to fill our shelves and thought perhaps you might be interested in selling old items you no longer want or plan to use."

Bonnie rolled her eyes and groaned. "I have a shed full. I'll have to take a look at what's out there. Perhaps you would like to stop by sometime next week?"

"Yes. If you don't mind. I almost forgot." Carlita pulled a card from her purse and handed it to Bonnie. "Call whenever you're ready. The next couple of days will be hectic for me, as well. We're unpacking inventory today and then tomorrow, my son is going to work on a small project in our basement. He's re-sealing a tunnel in our basement that connects with several others in the area."

Bonnie took the card. "Ah. Your place is over on Mulberry Street. An investigator Jackson something stopped by here a couple days ago. He wanted to inspect our tunnel to see if it connected to yours." She waved a hand. "Of course, the tunnels on this side of the street are gated so there's no way anyone could've gotten from our property to yours."

"You don't have a key?" Carlita asked.

"No." Bonnie shook her head. "I have no idea who installed the gate or who it even belongs to."

Carlita thanked Bonnie for her time and the woman promised to call in the next week or so, when she was ready to sort through the items in her shed. She walked Carlita to the front door and held it while Carlita stepped out onto the front porch.

"Thanks again." Carlita wandered down the steps and onto the sidewalk. "Someone has a key to that gate because they unlocked it. I heard them," she muttered to herself. Pirate Pete knew about the gate. Perhaps he was the one with the key.

She exited the property through the rear and passed by meticulously manicured gardens, complete with flowing fountains and a winding path, which led to a construction area.

She caught a glimpse of workers pouring concrete. A sign near the makeshift fence read 'Southern Serenity Pools.'

On her way home, Carlita passed by the Alder-Delaney place and could've sworn she caught a movement out of the corner of her eye but didn't dare glance in that direction. James Alder was a man with a chip on his shoulder and she'd decided it would be best to steer clear of her new neighbor.

She briefly wondered how much money the man would have to sink into the property. It would need a major overhaul, just like the Cobblestone place.

The gems Vinnie had left behind had been a godsend. She would never have gotten as far as she had on her own remodeling projects if not for the small bag of jewels.

When she reached the apartment, she made a beeline for the box of gems. Carlita hadn't looked inside the wooden box since the day she and her children found them in the basement.

Carlita dragged the box to the center of the living room and dropped to her knees as she lifted the lid. She propped the cover against the coffee table leg and leaned forward to inspect the contents.

The box was empty.

Chapter 23

Carlita's breath caught in her throat and the room began to spin. "Oh my gosh!" She shrieked as she jumped to her feet. She ran over to the other box, still sitting in the corner, ripped the lid off and peered inside. It was empty.

Had someone broken into their apartment and stolen the gems? They couldn't have. She hadn't told anyone about them.

Carlita ran to her daughter's bedroom. "Mercedes?" When she didn't answer, Carlita turned the knob and peeked inside. The room was empty.

"Tony?" Carlita hurried to check the rest of the apartment. Neither of her children was home.

She ran over to the fireplace and stuck her hand inside; fumbling around for the small bag of gems Vinnie had left behind. Carlita let out the breath she'd been holding when her fingers touched the velvet pouch.

Carlita jogged to the kitchen, pulled her cell phone from her purse and dialed Mercedes' cell phone.

"Hello?"

"Do you have the gems?" Carlita blurted out.

"No. They're in the same spot we've always kept them," Mercedes said.

"Not those. The *other* ones. The ones we found downstairs."

"No. They're in the box, right where we left them," Mercedes said.

"They're gone. I checked the boxes and they're empty."

"You're kidding," Mercedes said. "I'm on my way home. I'll be there in ten minutes. Where's Tony?"

"I don't know. I'm calling him next."

She disconnected the line and dialed her son's cell phone.

"Hello?"

"Where are you?"

"Unlocking the door to the apartment," Tony said.

The doorknob rattled and the door swung open. Tony stepped inside and ended the call. "What's up?"

"The gems! They're gone!" Carlita pointed at the empty boxes.

"You mean someone broke in and stole them?" Her son strode across the living room and peered into the box. "You didn't happen to move them?"

"No. Of course not!" Carlita's heart began to pound in her chest and she was certain she was on the verge of a nervous breakdown. "This is terrible."

Tony reached over and patted his mother's arm. "Nah! I moved them the other night. I was worried someone might break into the apartment. I figured if they're gutsy enough to wander around in our basement, what would stop them from breaking into our apartment?"

"You should've told me. I was freaking out."

"You shoulda seen the look on your face," Tony grinned but the grin quickly vanished at the look his mother gave him. "Sorry Ma. I was gonna tell you but I forgot. I stuck the tools and ledger in a box in the hall closet and hid the gems behind the fireplace mantle. Check this out."

Tony eased past his mother and stepped over to the fireplace. He grasped both ends and tugged. The entire mantle popped out, revealing a second shelf. Sitting on top of the hidden shelf was the large bag of gems as well as the smaller bag.

Mercedes blew through the door. "Does Tony know what happened to the gems?" she asked as she slammed the door behind her.

Carlita jabbed her finger at the mantle. "He hid them."

"Cool," Mercedes shifted the bag she was holding. "Way to give mom a coronary, bro!"

"I got the goods." Mercedes patted the shopping bag. "I looked all over. Best Bargain, Radio Shed. I even stopped by the flea markets downtown and no one had what I was looking for."

She reached into the bag and pulled out a small, round device. "I was on my way back here and decided to take a side street I'd never noticed before. I found this little oddities shop. It reminded me of a cross between an antique store and a pawnshop so I decided to check it out."

Mercedes handed the ball to Carlita. "This little old man, sweet as can be, showed me around. I told him about our pawnshop and that we were over on Mulberry Street and he said he knew who we were. Anyway, I told him I was looking for a small camera, something we could put in the hallway to keep an eye on our property and he showed me this."

Carlita turned it over in her hand. "Does it work?"

"Yep. Mr. Cuddahy showed me how to use it. He said he'd used it at his shop for a long time but recently upgraded. He wanted to add cameras outside and this one wasn't compatible with the newer models."

Carlita passed the camera to her son.

"It is such a cool place, cool and creepy." Mercedes reached into her pocket and pulled out a small business card. "Here's his card."

Carlita's eyes squinted as she studied the small print on the card. "Oddities and Antiquities. A shop for all ages." The card was a cream color and the corners jagged. It looked old. "I'll have to stop by there one of these days."

She handed the card to her daughter. "In the meantime, I don't know about you, but I'm starving. I have a whole dish of leftover bowtie pasta I can throw in the oven to warm up while we set the trap. Give me five minutes." Carlita hurried to the kitchen, turned the oven on and pulled the dish of leftovers from the refrigerator.

She freshened up in the bathroom and when she emerged, the oven had warmed. Carlita slid the casserole dish into the oven and then knocked on Mercedes' bedroom door.

The door abruptly opened. "I was testing the camera again to make sure we can loop the recording and also watch it live. It works like a charm. This is the best fifty bucks I've spent in a long time."

"You paid fifty bucks for that?" Carlita frowned.

"It was worth every penny. We can use it in the pawnshop when we're done or even up here to keep an eye on the outer hall."

"We'll leave the bargaining to your brother," Carlita teased.

Tony was waiting for them downstairs and Carlita and Mercedes hurried to join him. The trio descended the ladder and made their way into the basement.

Carlita glanced at the tunnel. "I can't wait to seal this shut."

Mercedes, who had purchased a small bracket and screws to attach the camera, climbed halfway up the ladder and picked what she deemed the perfect spot to install the small device.

She screwed the brackets in place and positioned the camera so that it faced the tunnel. After making a couple small adjustments, she hopped off the ladder. "Perfect. Now all we have to do is wait for someone to show up."

Tony reached into his front pocket and pulled out a small blue stone. He turned it over in his hand. "I'm gonna use this as bait. It will keep the intruder snooping around long enough to call the cops, unless you want me to handle it?"

Carlita was already shaking her head. "No. I don't want you to handle it. If we see something, we call. We'll have to take shifts watching the camera."

"I'll take the first shift," Carlita said. "Otherwise I might fall asleep at the wheel."

"I'll take the second," Tony said. "I figure late night/early morning is the most likely time the intruder will make an appearance."

"I'll take the third shift since I'm a night owl," Mercedes said.

Tony, Mercedes and Carlita ascended the ladder. They waited for Tony to replace the trap door before heading back upstairs.

"Don't those cameras have some sort of infrared ray?" Carlita asked.

"Yeah, but it's not very bright and I doubt whoever it is will be looking for a camera," Mercedes said.

Tony stopped in the hall outside the apartment. "I'm gonna stop by Shelby's place to say hello. Don't wait for me. Go ahead and eat dinner."

Mercedes and Carlita headed into the apartment and closed the door.

Carlita leaned against the closed door and peeked through the peephole.

"Stop spying on them," Mercedes said.

"You're right. I should mind my own business." Carlita stepped away from the door and Mercedes took her place.

"Hey!" Carlita said.

"What? I'm just taking a quick glance," Mercedes said. She took a step back. "They went inside and closed the door."

Tony still hadn't returned by the time the leftovers had warmed so mother and daughter ate without him, all the while discussing the probability of catching the intruder in the act.

"I did everything I could. I told them how we'd found not only the skeletal remains but something else and I was anxious to re-seal the tunnel." Carlita told her daughter about her brief conversation with John Alder and how rude he'd been.

"Hopefully he mellows out before he opens his bed and breakfast," Mercedes said.

"I thought the same thing." Carlita told her Pirate Pete had asked when they were stopping by for dinner and then told her of meeting Bonnie Aberdeen. "Both of them said they would let me know when they were ready to get rid of some of their stuff."

Mercedes stabbed a bowtie pasta and nibbled the edge. "The bed and breakfast had some cool stuff. I bet the Parrot House Restaurant does, too."

They had already finished their food and cleared the table by the time Tony returned. "Sorry Ma. Shelby made a pot roast and invited me to stay. I should've let you know," he said guiltily.

"No problem. There's still some left for a midnight snack if you want to munch on it during your shift."

It had been a long day and Carlita was whupped. Rambo, on the other hand, wasn't having any of that. "Rambo needs to go out."

"I'll take him," Tony said. "Let's go Rambo." Rambo and Tony exited the apartment. Mercedes headed to her room while Carlita set up a command center at the dining room table.

Rambo and Tony returned a short time later and Tony headed to Carlita's bedroom to take a nap while she slid into the chair and stared at the dark screen. Her eyelids were already growing heavy and keeping both eyes focused on a blank screen didn't help. She began to doze off and then jumped to her feet. "Time for coffee." She made a fresh pot and then settled in a second time. It was going to be a long night.

Chapter 24

Carlita stared at the screen until she thought she'd have to prop her eyelids open with toothpicks.

Finally, Tony emerged from the bedroom, ready to start his shift.

"It's quiet as a mouse down there," Carita reported as she eased out of the chair and stretched her stiff joints. "I hope something happens soon."

"I figured you wouldn't see anything. You've gotta give the criminal element a chance to get on their game."

"I hope you're right," Carlita lifted her hands above her head and stretched. "I left some coffee in the pot. You'll need to nuke it, though. It's cold."

"Thanks Ma."

Carlita squeezed Tony's shoulder and turned to go.

"Sorry about the gem scare earlier," Tony apologized. "I forgot."

"It's okay son," Carlita said. "We've had a lot going on. Speaking of a lot going on, you heard from your brother Vinnie yet?"

"Oh yeah!" Tony snapped his fingers. "He said he's almost positive the coast is clear so he'll be leaving Jersey soon and heading down here."

"We'll have a full house. I'll run to the store tomorrow to pick up an air mattress," Carlita said. "Bob Lowman will be here in the morning to go over plans for your apartment."

She didn't wait for a reply as she shuffled to her bedroom. Carlita had just crawled into bed when she heard a shout coming from the other room.

"We got a live one!"

Carlita flung the covers back and ran into the dining room. Mercedes was right behind her.

Mother and daughter leaned over Tony's shoulder. They watched as a small light bobbed up and down. The light grew brighter before it began bouncing around the basement.

"I hope they don't spot the camera," Mercedes whispered.

"Me too," Carlita said.

The beam of light shifted and then dropped to the floor. They watched as a dark shadow flitted back and forth.

"When do we move in for the kill?" Mercedes asked.

"Give em a few minutes to start digging," Tony said. "I have a little surprise I didn't tell you about. Earlier, I rigged up an extension cord and placed a utility light in the corner, near the tunnel entrance. The switch is near the trap door. I figured at the right moment, we flip the switch and flood the place with bright light. Hopefully, the intruder becomes disoriented long enough for me to yank the trap door off and catch them in the act."

"But first we call the cops," Carlita said. "And I'm doing that right now." She dialed the 911 number and told the dispatcher someone was in her basement.

After the dispatcher promised to send a car right away, Carlita ended the call and the trio hurried into the hall and down the stairs. They raced into the back room of the pawnshop.

Mercedes reached for the light switch.

Tony grabbed the handle of the trap door. "One…two…three…!"

Tony yanked the trap door open. Mercedes flipped the switch while Tony scrambled down the ladder gun in hand. "Stop right where you are!" he shouted.

The perpetrator, blinded by the bright light, crashed into the brick wall, lurched backward and then fell to the ground.

"Drop the shovel! Now!" Tony shouted as he pointed his gun at the petite woman sitting on the floor.

The sound of police sirens filled the air and Carlita caught a glimpse of the cruiser's bubble light through the alley window. She ran to the door to let them in and then led them to the basement.

The two officers descended the ladder. One of the officers reached down and grabbed the arm of a scowling Bonnie Aberdeen.

"I knew it!" Mercedes said.

The officers led Bonnie up the ladder and to the waiting patrol car.

While one of the officers placed the woman in the back of the patrol car, the other officer turned to Carlita. "What happened?"

Carlita briefly explained how they'd set up a surveillance camera after discovering someone was sneaking into their basement. "The woman, Bonnie Aberdeen, owns Cobblestone Bed & Breakfast and we believe she was sneaking in through an underground tunnel that connects our properties."

"Give me a few minutes," the officer told his partner. He turned to Carlita. "Show me the tunnel."

She led him back down into the basement and through the tunnel. Tony and Mercedes, still in the basement, followed behind.

When they reached the gate, they noticed it was ajar. The officer pushed the gate all the way open and they continued walking until they reached a fork in the tunnel. "You mentioned the woman owns Cobblestone Bed & Breakfast. Do you know which direction that might be?"

"This way." Mercedes pointed to the left. "Follow me."

They turned left and continued walking until finally reaching a set of brick steps. "If my calculations are correct, Cobblestone's pantry is at the top of these stairs."

The officer, followed by Carlita, Mercedes and Tony, crept up the steps. When they reached the top, they came face-to-face with a man wearing wire-rimmed glasses and a bathrobe. "Where's my wife?"

"She's sitting in my patrol car, waiting to be taken down to the police station. She's being charged with trespassing," the officer replied.

"Trespassing? She was down in our basement," the man huffed.

"Down in *our* basement," Tony said.

Mr. Aberdeen, Bonnie's husband, let loose a string of expletives and then calmed down long enough to tell them he would be contacting an attorney right after he posted his wife's bail.

The police officer, along with Mercedes, Tony and Carlita retraced their steps as they made their way back to their basement.

"Technically we can't charge her with breaking and entering," the officer said. "We could get her for trespassing."

He shifted to the side. "I can't say as she broke any other law. Digging around in someone else's dirt isn't much of a crime."

When they reached the metal gate, the officer pulled the gate shut. "I've always heard a lot of unusual activity goes on down here, right under our feet."

Carlita, Mercedes and Tony showed the officer the looped video of Bonnie Aberdeen entering the basement. He asked Mercedes to forward a copy to his email and then made his way to the waiting patrol car.

Carlita watched the patrol car back out of the alley and onto the street before she closed the back door. "I guess we won't be buying any antiques from the Aberdeens." She turned to her daughter. "You said you had a suspect in mind. Was Bonnie your suspect?"

"Yep," Mercedes nodded. "Think about it. Her property accesses this area. Where did she come up with all the money to reno that beautiful bed and breakfast? I think she found a gem, just like Elvira did the other day. She got to digging around and found several other gems inside the tunnel, probably some that had dropped along the way to being transported to the river."

Carlita picked up. "After the police questioned her about the body in the tunnel, she must've realized we'd removed the wall so she decided to search our property as well."

"And she would've hit the jackpot had it not been for the fact we got to the gems first," Tony said.

"I thought for sure it was John Alder," Carlita said. "He seems so angry."

"Maybe he was having a bad day," Mercedes started up the steps to the apartment. "You should give him a second chance."

"You're right Mercedes," Carlita said. "I think I will. Everyone deserves a second chance."

Chapter 25

Carlita awoke early the next morning. After all the excitement of the previous night, she figured she wouldn't be able to sleep a wink, but sleep came easily and before she knew it, rays of morning light were beaming in through the gap in her bedroom curtains.

The first thing she thought of was Bonnie Aberdeen. The second thing she thought of was having Tony seal the tunnel and the third, most important thing that came to mind was her son Vinnie would be there soon!

She hurried to the bathroom, showered, dressed and headed to the kitchen.

Tony was out on the deck with Rambo. He turned as his mother opened the slider. "Wow! You're up and at 'em early today."

"We have a lot to do." She ticked off her mental to-do list. "I need to pick up an air mattress. We need work on store inventory. We need..."

"Coffee," Tony groaned. "First we need coffee."

While the coffee brewed, Carlita sliced the pumpkin bread she'd picked up at Colby's Corner store during her last visit. "Don't forget Bob Lowman will be by today to discuss the renovations to your apartment."

"Yep." Tony nodded and reached for a clean coffee cup. "You sure know how to stay busy."

"It helps keep me out of trouble."

After they finished their snack and coffee, Tony headed to the bathroom to get ready since his to-do list was the longest.

At ten o'clock, when Mercedes still hadn't emerged from her bedroom, Carlita tapped on her bedroom door and stuck her head around the corner. "Hey there, sleepyhead."

"There oughta be a law against being chipper this early." Mercedes groaned and pulled the covers over her head.

"It's after ten," Carlita said.

"Like I said, there oughta be a law. I'm up, I'm up."

After straightening the kitchen, Carlita took Rambo for a long walk. Soon, her place would be a madhouse with three of her four children camping out in the cozy two-bedroom apartment.

She passed John Alder's place on the way to the park and noticed a large piece of furniture blocking part of the front window. Carlita picked up the pace, anxious to avoid another confrontation with her new neighbor.

They turned the corner and Carlita shivered as a cool morning breeze blew off the river. Rambo and Carlita hurried across the busy street and made their way to a nearby bench. She was thankful she'd remembered to bring her sweater and tugged it tight against her frame as she settled onto the bench to watch Rambo sniff the bushes nearby.

"Hello."

A male voice echoed in her ear and Carlita turned to see who it was.

John Alder stepped closer. He waved at an empty section of bench. "Do you mind?"

"No. Not at all," Carlita said as she scooched to the right to make room for him.

"It's going to be a beautiful day. I forgot how much I loved certain parts of Savannah." He eased onto the bench and placed his elbows on the top of his knees.

Rambo trotted over to greet the man and John patted his head. "Pretty dog."

"Thanks. He's a character."

John leaned back as Rambo moved on. "I was going to drop by your place later today to thank you for the cupcakes. They were delicious. I also wanted to apologize for my rude behavior."

"It's okay. We all have bad days," Carlita said graciously. "You did ruffle my feathers, though, especially when you called me out on the snooping part."

She glanced at him out of the corner of her eye. There were deep creases between his eyes and around his forehead. Worry lines, Carlita liked to call them. His hair, a shade of sandy brown was sprinkled with touches of gray.

His green eyes, when they met hers, held more than a hint of sadness. "I bet you're wondering why I would buy back the old home after all these years."

"A little," Carlita admitted.

He shrugged. "Sometimes I wonder myself. It looks like fate stepped in." John clasped his hands together. "An Investigator, Patrick Jackson, stopped by today. The final autopsy results came in and a second medical examiner looked at the skeletal remains found near your property. There was a small chip on one of the teeth and Jackson asked if I remembered my mother having a chipped front tooth."

Carlita shifted on the bench. "And?"

"She did. Even though I was young when my mother disappeared, I remember several injuries...incidents. One day she was okay and the next, her hand was bandaged, sometimes there were bruises on her arms. She'd also chipped one of her front teeth, not long before she disappeared."

"Your father physically abused your mother," Carlita said softly. "Did you think she ran off when she disappeared?"

"At first. That's what dad told us, but over the years I began to question the reasoning. My mother was a loving mother. She would never have abandoned my sister and me." John sucked in a deep breath. "So it looks like I made it home just in time to put her to rest, once and for all."

Carlita's throat squeezed shut at the thought of an abusive man who murdered his wife. She thought about the guilt the children must have felt, perhaps even unloved enough for a mother to abandon them.

She said the only thing she could. "I'm so sorry."

"Thank you." John rose to his feet. "And again, I am sorry. Can we start over?" He reached down for Carlita's hand.

She smiled and stuck her hand in his. "Absolutely. I'm a big believer in new beginnings."

He offered her his arm. "Can I walk you home?"

"I would like that John. I would like that very much." Carlita linked her arm in John's arm and with Rambo leading the way, the two of them headed back to Walton Square…home.

Two weeks later.

Carlita shaded her eyes and studied the sign out front, '*Savannah Swag Pawn Shop.*' "Are you sure customers aren't going to get the wrong impression on the name, Savannah Swag? I mean, I don't want anyone to think we're pedaling stolen goods."

"You worry too much," Vinnie said. "It's an awesome name, a real attention grabber. We're gonna be so busy, the cops'll have to start directing traffic out front."

Vinnie, Jr., Carlita's oldest son, had arrived in town several days earlier. With the help of Vinnie, Tony and Mercedes, the Garlucci family had finished all of the projects necessary to get their pawnshop up and running. The long-awaited moment had finally arrived. They were ready to open for business.

Autumn had managed to squeeze in a small news article, announcing the grand opening of Savannah Swag Pawn Shop. They'd also been advertising the grand opening in several online ads.

Everything was ready. The balloons were in place, the coffee fresh and hot, batches of homemade cookies baked and some spectacular giveaways lined up. Now all they needed were customers.

"I hope you're right." Carlita took one last look at the new sign and then made her way to the front door and the sign hanging in the front window. She flipped the sign over to read, *Open*.

Carlita linked arms with Vinnie and they made their way inside the store. "I sometimes wondered if this day would ever come but thanks to the help of my family, my children, I've finally become an independent woman. I can't wait to see what my future holds."

The end.

Made in Savannah Series
Book #5…coming soon!

Get Free Books and More

Get free and discounted books, giveaways & soon-to-be-released books, when you sign up for my Free Cozy Mysteries Newsletter.

HopeCallaghan.com/newsletter

Meet The Author

Hope Callaghan is an author who loves to write Christian books, especially Christian Mystery and Cozy Mystery books. She has written more than 45 mystery books (and counting) in five series.

Born and raised in a small town in West Michigan, she now lives in Florida with her husband.

She is the proud mother of one daughter and a stepdaughter and stepson. When she's not doing the thing she loves best - writing books - she enjoys cooking, traveling and reading books.

Hope loves to connect with her readers! Connect with her today!

Visit hopecallaghan.com for special offers, free books, and soon-to-be-released books!

Email: hope@hopecallaghan.com

Facebook: https://www.facebook.com/hopecallaghanauthor/

Bow Tie Pasta with Sausage, Tomatoes and Cream Recipe

Ingredients:

1 (12 ounce) package bow tie pasta
2 tablespoons olive oil
1 pound spicy Italian sausage, crumbled (can substitute turkey sausage)
*½ tsp. red pepper flakes (OPTIONAL)
½ cup diced yellow onion
3 cloves garlic, minced
1 (28 ounce) can Italian-style tomatoes
1-1/2 cups heavy cream
½ tsp. salt
¼ cup green olives, chopped
2 tsps. Garlucci family secret Sicilian seasoning
1 cup Italian blend cheese (OPTIONAL)

Directions

-Bring large pot of slightly salted water to a boil. Cook pasta 8 – 10 minutes, until al dente. Drain.

- While pasta is cooking, heat oil in large skillet over medium heat. Cook sausage and (optional) red pepper flakes until sausage is browned. Drain grease if necessary.
- Stir in onion and garlic until onion is lightly browned.
- Stir in tomatoes, cream, salt, green olives and Carlita's secret Sicilian seasoning.
-Simmer until mixture thickens, 8 – 10 minutes.

*Alternative recipe:

-While mixture simmers, preheat oven to 350 degrees.
- After mixture thickens, add ½ cup Italian blend cheese, pour into 9x13 glass baking dish. Top with ½ cup Italian cheese blend and bake for 15 minutes, or until cheese melts.

*The red pepper flakes add a bit of heat so if you don't like spicy foods, skip this ingredient.

Garlucci Family Secret Sicilian Seasoning Recipe

Ingredients:

2 tablespoons dried basil
2 tablespoons dried oregano
2 tablespoons dried marjoram
2 tablespoons dried thyme
2 tablespoons dried savory
1 tablespoons dried rosemary
1 tablespoons dried sage

Blend for one minute in food processor. Store in dry container.

Made in the USA
Columbia, SC
18 March 2022